"**This is your last chance, Bryce,**" Ellis said, standing by his bed. "**You act like a man and use this salve, or I'm washing my hands of you.**"

"Oh, Ellis," he muttered, a mischievous twinkle in his eye. "Asking me to slather that stuff on my body is like asking me to slit my own wrists. Don't go thinking I'm unmanly or ungrateful. I just can't do it myself." He pushed the sheets low and pulled his T-shirt high on his chest. "But I'd sit quiet and let you do it."

Her eyes lowered to the great expanse of warm, golden flesh over tight, rippling muscles. She swallowed hard, then met the challenge in his eyes. Her hands trembled when she grabbed a handful of the mixture and brought her fingers slowly to his chest.

Bryce sucked in air as if he'd been burnt. She pulled back and glanced up. His gaze met and captured hers, fire and passion flaming within him. Unbearable heat scorched her in a stare that held her locked in place, a willing prisoner.

Her heart raced hard and fast; her breathing was ragged and irregular. Her whole body trembled when he took her hand in his and slowly lowered it back to his chest, near the steady pounding of his heart. Waves of desire passed from his body to hers, charging her with excitement and need.

He raised his other hand from the bed, and she felt his fingers caress her cheek, gently, tenderly, as if she might break. She felt cherished and adored.

His fingers traced the outline of her jaw, then traced a path of rapture down the column of her neck. "Ellis," he whispered softly. "I'm gonna kiss you. . . ."

WHAT ARE *LOVESWEPT* ROMANCES?

They are stories of true romance and touching emotion. We believe those two very important ingredients are constants in our highly sensual and very believable stories in the *LOVESWEPT* line. Our goal is to give you, the reader, stories of consistently high quality that may sometimes make you laugh, sometimes make you cry, but are always fresh and creative and contain many delightful surprises within their pages.

Most romance fans read an enormous number of books. Those they truly love, they keep. Others may be traded with friends and soon forgotten. We hope that each *LOVESWEPT* romance will be a treasure—a "keeper." We will always try to publish

LOVE STORIES YOU'LL NEVER FORGET
BY AUTHORS YOU'LL ALWAYS REMEMBER

The Editors

Mary Kay McComas
Sweet Dreamin' Baby

BANTAM BOOKS
NEW YORK · TORONTO · LONDON · SYDNEY · AUCKLAND

SWEET DREAMIN' BABY

A Bantam Book / May 1992

If you would be interested in receiving protective vinyl
covers for your Loveswept books, please write to this address
for information:

Loveswept
Bantam Books
P.O. Box 985
Hicksville, NY 11802

ISBN 0-553-44210-4

Published simultaneously in the United States and Canada

PRINTED IN THE UNITED STATES OF AMERICA

OPM   0 9 8 7 6 5 4 3 2 1

One

Webster, Kentucky, wasn't much of a town. But the roads were paved, the people were somewhat friendly, and it was as far away from Stony Hollow as Ellis could get on sixteen dollars and eleven cents worth of gas.

Jobs were scarce. Most folks worked in the mill a few miles down the road. Ellis, too, had asked for work at Webster Textiles. Her name had been added to a long waiting list for the first unskilled job opening. With her employment opportunities suddenly narrowed to a fine line and her pockets near empty, she was grateful for the part-time work she'd been given at the tavern—a popular place called the Steel Wheel.

But it wasn't enough. Ellis needed money. Lots of money. And she needed it as soon as she could get it.

She leaned against the bar, her problems heavy in her heart. She'd been lonely and poor most of her life, but she'd never felt more alone or desperate. She tapped the plastic serving tray with her thumbnail and chewed her lower lip. She wasn't earning the money fast enough. What she needed was a second job, she decided. She'd start looking for one the next morning.

"These here bottles ain't goin' to walk over to them tables, little girl," Tug Hogan said in a matter-of-fact manner, barely glancing at her before moving down the bar to replenish another beer. The big, burly man was the owner and only bartender of the Steel Wheel. From the beginning he'd warned her that if she couldn't keep up with the quick, steady pace of taking orders and delivering drinks to his customers, he'd let her go. It was a threat that brought terror to the pit of her stomach.

She didn't approve of the imbibing of bottled spirits for other than medicinal purposes, and it scuffed against her grain to be working in a place where they flowed so freely. But her circumstances had taken her beyond caring. A job was a job after all, and she was eager to keep it.

She hastily put the five tall bottles of beer on her tray and carefully maneuvered her way around tables and patrons to a gathering of three men and a solitary drinker at the back of the bar near one of the two pool tables.

The front door of the bar burst open and a rush of icy October wind assaulted the back of her neck, sweeping a chill into the warmth she'd finally accumulated inside her pullover sweater. She glanced absently at the offender, a tall young man who presently began to respond to a handful of casual greetings. She shivered and hoped he wouldn't dawdle before he closed the door.

She blinked as he turned toward her, a beam of dim light defining his features. She did an immediate double take. Her lips parted in a silent gasp. She stared as a strange tightness gripped her low in the abdomen and her heart began to flutter erratically about in her chest. He was as big as life and twice as natural.

She gaped openly at his well-formed frame, at the broad shoulders that filled the thick flannel shirt and quilted vest; at the slim hips and muscled thighs wrapped comfortably in blue denim. It was his face, however, that held her attention. There was no denying his strong, handsome features. He had the look of a man who plowed straight furrows and went to the end of each row, someone honest and dependable. But there was also the mien of a rounder, a pistol, a card, a fun-loving fellow. And tying the two together was a calm, quiet gentleness that made her efforts to swallow her amazement rather difficult. He smiled at someone, and her breath caught in her throat.

"Hillbilly!"

The name jolted Ellis from her reverie and forcefully brought to mind her reasons for being where she was. Ridiculous rubbish. She didn't have the time to be taken by a man's good looks. With a quick peek at Tug Hogan she reminded herself of how dearly she needed to keep her job, of how little time she had to earn a great deal of money, and of how much she loved what she'd left behind in Stony Hollow.

She looked at the man who had called out to her. He was narrow eyed and looked like forty miles of rough road.

"You gonna stand there all day?" he asked, elbowing one of the three men at the table next to his when he noticed her discomfort. "Hillbillies don't know if they're comin', goin', or standin' still."

"Shut up, Reuben," one of the other men said, offering Ellis an apologetic smile. His face looked slightly familiar to her, but like everyone else in the dimly lit, smoke-filled room, he was a stranger to her.

More accurately, she was a stranger to them. In the two weeks she had been in Webster, she'd hardly said more than one word at a time to anyone. She'd learned early that the less you said, the less you were noticed, and the less you were noticed, the less people bothered you. But it didn't appear to apply to newcomers in small towns. Ellis's silence actually generated curiosity in the townspeople, and her continued reticence brought forth a mixture of attitudes toward her.

She set one of the beers on the table in front of the man who'd called her a hillbilly and turned to set the others before the man who'd tried to apologize, without a direct look at either of them. She didn't mind being called a hillbilly. Truth was, she was a hillbilly. But she did mind the term being used as an insult—and she hated it when the expression invoked pity.

"Howdy, brother," a humor-filled voice came from directly behind her. "Does your wife know where you are?"

"Of course," said the man who had smiled at Ellis. "She gave me just enough money for two beers and told me to have a good time."

All the men laughed as if it were a very good joke before the man called Reuben spoke again.

"What kinda man needs his ol' lady's permission to have a few beers? Never thought I'd live to see the day when a good ol' boy like Buck LaSalle would be abendin' hisself like a pretzel for a female," he said, unaware of the ominous stillness around him.

Ellis set the last beer in front of Buck LaSalle and lifted her gaze in apprehension, knowing what alcohol could do to a man's temper. He surprised her with a good-humored wink. At the same time the man behind her laughed.

"There ain't a man in three counties who wouldn't give his right arm to have Anne for his wife, and you know it, Reuben Evans," he said. "And if you're here lookin' to raise a breeze with a LaSalle, you'd best address yourself to me, not to my brother."

Ellis couldn't help turning to look at the young man she'd seen moments earlier standing in the doorway, nor could she keep her knees steady when she did. She glanced back at Buck and saw the strong resemblance between the two.

Buck LaSalle's brother was as tall as a steeple. She had to tilt her chin upward to look at his face. He wasn't the least bit put out with Reuben Evans; his personable expression was mild and leaning to lighthearted. She might have doubted his challenging words if she hadn't heard the rancorous undertones in his voice.

"No call to get on your high horse, Bryce," Reuben Evans said, not quite able to look him in the eye as he spoke. He took a long gulp of beer. "It's no skin off my nose if your brother wants to spend the rest of his life with a ring through his. I just think a woman oughta know her place." He stood then and came nose to chin with Bryce. Fixing him with a pointed stare, he added, "Like my Liddy."

Ellis watched as Bryce's spine grew as stiff as a stick and his eyes became bright with anger. She'd heard bits and pieces of the Reuben and Liddy Evans story that involved Bryce LaSalle. Reuben had run out on Liddy and their three children over two and a half years earlier, and Bryce had stepped in to take his place for a while. Bryce, Liddy, and the children had become kin in the eyes of the community, all but for a divorce and new marriage ceremony. Then, rather abruptly and without public explanation, they'd split the sheets and gone their separate ways. Tongues wagged furiously whenever they met in public and were still affectionate and friendly.

The people of Webster had grown to accept their new relationship as well, until Reuben had returned several months later. He'd been greeted with every obvious detail of the goings on between his wife and Bryce LaSalle during his absence. When Liddy had refused to accept him back into his own home and continued to turn to Bryce for . . . well, for whatever she turned to Bryce for, Reuben had drawn his own conclusions as to the not-so-obvious details of their relationship.

An odd pang of . . . something registered in Ellis's mind. She hardly knew these people, and she certainly didn't care about them. Still, she felt a sort of empathy for Liddy Evans and quite honestly approved of her choice between the two men.

Reuben half turned back to the table for another gulp of beer, keeping a wary eye on his wife's former lover. He wiped his mouth on his sleeve, saying, "My Liddy's still tryin' to bust my chops for cuttin' out on her, but she ain't stupid." He caught sight of Ellis and muttered,

"She ain't no hillbilly girl neither. She'll come around soon enough. She knows her place."

Ellis, Bryce, and the three men seated at the table watched as he sauntered away. He paid no heed to those he nudged or bumped into on his way to the door.

"Sit on down, Bryce," Buck said.

"Sorry piece of work there," one of the other men commented, referring to Evans. The last man added, "If his brain was in a bird's head, the bird'd fly backwards."

Bryce brought his gaze from the door to the table as an easy grin took its rightful place in his expression.

"He missed a mighty fine supper tonight," he said, and a unified groan rose from the table.

"Ya didn't go over there again, did ya?" Buck asked harshly, his disapproval clear.

"Yep." Bryce sat down at the table, pushing a half-finished beer away from him. "And I'll keep on goin' till I'm sure he's doin' right by Liddy and the boys."

"She's not your concern anymore." Buck's tone told of his own concern for his brother.

"She'll always be my concern," he said simply, looking at Ellis—actually seeing her for the first time. His face lit up like a new saloon.

Small and frail, holding her head high with an unconscious air of pride and elegance, the girl had a face that reminded Bryce of one of those special angels he'd seen pictures of in the family bible—a seraph. The dim overhead lighting reflected off her blond locks, creating a golden halo around her head. And when she angled herself just so, he could see that her eyes were bluer than the sky. Lord, she was pretty. She looked like an angel who'd just stepped off the bus from heaven.

He smiled at her and asked, "That one mine?"

"What?"

He was pointing to the fourth beer she'd brought to the table, plainly ordered in anticipation of his arrival.

"That one mine?" he asked again, the same faint

lights showing his hazel eyes to be as green and gold and warm as an Indian summer.

It occurred to all of them at once that her continued presence at their table was highly inappropriate considering the exchange of hard spirits that had just transpired. She'd never been a barmaid before, but she was fully aware that she should have left the drinks and disappeared as any good barmaid would have. To be standing in the middle of a personal upscuddle between two patrons . . . well, to be standing in the middle of anything that didn't concern her was incredibly rude.

Self-conscious in the extreme, she nodded, picked up the beer, and set it in front of him. She started to leave.

"I heard ol' Tug hired himself a pretty little gal with eyes the color of bluebells and hair as bright and shiny as a field full of buttercups," she heard Bryce say. "You must be Ellen."

She turned to see the other men at the table smiling perceptively and lowering their eyes as if they were reluctant to witness an awkward, intimate moment between two strangers. She looked then at Bryce and was startled to see the appreciation in his eyes. It made her feel like she had a belly full of ants.

"I'm Bryce LaSalle," he said, his voice deep and soft. "You know my brother Buck?"

She shook her head and nodded at Buck, then nodded again and once more as she followed his introductions around the table. "Jim Doles. Pete Harper."

"Ellis," she said after a moment of uncertain silence. "My name is Ellis."

"Where are you from, Ellis?" Buck asked. Bryce had taken to staring at her.

"Stony Hollow. This side of Magoffin County." It might have been a leftover reaction to Reuben Evans or it might have been her aversion to revealing even the simplest facts about herself to anyone, but for a moment Ellis thought she saw a knowing look in the men's eyes, a knowledge of where and what she came from and who she was.

"I'm a hillbilly," she said proudly, feeling an urge to defend the term before they could sully it.

"Hell, aren't we all?" Buck asked, laughing as the others joined in his amusement.

The others, that is, except Bryce, who watched her with open interest. She'd made her simple declaration with such composure and dignity that it sent chills up his spine—like hearing the national anthem on the Fourth of July.

"Some of us are more hillbilly than others," she said softly.

What Buck had said was true enough. To the world in general anyone living in the heart of the Appalachian Mountains was a hillbilly. But among themselves, there was a distinction between the country folk who lived close to the coal mining or textile towns and in the farming communities, and those who had settled in small hollows and pockets of the mountains nearly two hundred years earlier—those who had kept to themselves and refused to embrace modernization.

Ellis wasn't one of those descendants by blood, but mountain life was so much a part of her that she might as well have been. She was poor and not as well educated as some, but she had no shame for the fact.

She lifted her chin and dared any one of the men before her to comment on the differences between them.

"Will you be wantin' anythin' else?" she asked, her defiant gaze coming to rest on Bryce, who felt a lifting surge in his midsection. What a magnificent creature she was. Small in stature, pure and innocent of face . . . and yet she had more might and power in her mettle than any ten men of his acquaintance.

"No, ma'am. No, thank you," he said, a curious expression on his face, unsure of how to approach her.

"Holler if ya do," she said. She turned and walked

back to the bar feeling almost brave for the first time since she'd left Stony Hollow.

She missed feeling as if she had solid ground beneath her. In Stony Hollow she'd been deliberate in her acts and intentions. Survival was another lesson she'd learned early. She could remember years of feeling confused and helpless, times when she had no control over her life. But that hadn't been the case since . . . well, for a long time now, she thought, recalling the exact moment she'd taken control of her destiny.

She smiled over a precious memory.

"You caught up?" Tug asked in his gruff, indifferent manner.

"Yes, sir," she said, glancing quickly at the tables she'd been waiting on to make sure.

"Haul a Miller keg out and fill the racks then."

"Yes, sir," she said without hesitating. Taking orders with no please or thank you or intonation of goodwill was something she was accustomed to. Moving heavy objects and working in the cold were not new to her either.

As a matter of fact, she preferred the mindless manual labor to waiting on the customers. It gave her more time to think and plan, and she didn't have to be polite or answer questions.

What had that Bryce fellah said? she ruminated as she entered the cold storage behind the bar. That he'd heard Ol' Tug had hired a new barmaid? She wondered how many other people had heard the same thing. Did the whole town know that someone new was working at the Steel Wheel? Would they be free with the information if someone—say, another stranger in town—happened to ask?

Again, a sense of urgency overcame her as she twisted a heavy keg of beer to the cooler door. She was going to have to work harder and faster at getting the money she needed, she decided resolutely. *Bryce La-Salle.* His name fluttered through her mind like a butterfly, sunny and springlike. No. She couldn't think about him. There was something about him that pleased her, but she couldn't let him clutter her mind. Not now. Maybe someday, after she had her money and after she was safe and settled, if he were still around . . .

"Can I help ya with that?"

"What?" Already breathless from exertion, she nearly jumped out of her skin at the sound of Bryce's voice. "No," she blurted out, looking in her employer's direction. "I can do it."

"Let me help. It's too heavy for you."

"No it ain't." She went back to turning and twisting the keg toward the bar.

"Hell, ya ain't any bigger than a minute. You'll break your back doin' that."

For no other reason than that he was a customer and she had to be nice to him, she said, "Thank ya for offerin', but I can do it."

"I don't mind." He really didn't. He was eager to find an excuse to learn more about her.

"I do," she muttered under a grunt of energy. More clearly she added, "I don't want your help, Mr. LaSalle. I can do just fine without it."

"There's a difference between wantin' and needin', ya know," he said. Any other female he knew would have batted her eyes, giggled, and stepped aside to let him herniate himself with the beer keg. Ellis's refusal was disconcerting.

She turned on him with the words to tell him that she neither wanted nor needed any help from him on the tip of her tongue, when she suddenly recalled where she was.

"Please," she said, pleading with him. "Let me do my job."

As before, he wore a curious expression as he studied her. He took a step backward, his hands held out in defeat. "Sorry," he said. "I didn't mean any harm."

She wanted to call out to him as he walked back to his table. She wanted to explain how important her job was and how much she needed the money she was earning. She hadn't meant to offend him. Thinking about it, she couldn't recollect that anyone had ever offered to perform a chore for her before. He was a strange man, she speculated, turning back to her task with a odd sensation of warmth in her chest.

Bryce was confused . . . and dismayed. How was he going to get to talk with her if she wouldn't have anything to do with him, wouldn't even let him break his back for her? Since Buck was permanently out of the picture with his marriage to Anne, and few others could hold a candle to the LaSalle brothers in charm, wit, and good looks, the dating game in Webster had been played primarily in Bryce's ball park. He was used to the contestants lining up to take their turn at him, all hoping to be the grand winner. So, why didn't Ellis want to play?

He didn't speak to her again, except to murmur a thank you when she delivered the next round of drinks to his table later in the night. But he did continue to bother her.

She couldn't count the times her gaze wandered back to his table to find him watching her. He was very handsome. Her face and neck would grow warm, her hands would tremble, and her insides would tie themselves in knots. She felt nervous and excited at once. He disturbed her in the oddest manner. And she couldn't say she didn't enjoy it. Wondering about what he was like, what he thought about, and what it would be like if he touched her took her mind off her problems for whole periods of time that were like minivacations. Refreshing and invigorating.

But her problems far outweighed the pleasure his attention and her fantasies brought her. All too quickly they dispelled her notions of feeling silly and happy and young. All too quickly they would call forth the worry, the struggle, and the strife that were her life.

It was a physical relief to see him leave with his brother and friends shortly before the bar closed for the night. The emotional bouncing between giddy and guilty was exhausting. She was convinced that once he was out of her sight she could concentrate on one thing at a time—the one thing she needed to concentrate on—money.

"Come an hour early tomorrow and clean out the back room," Tug Hogan told her, as she pulled her thick woolen coat over her shoulders, getting ready to leave.

"Yes, sir." She was glad for the extra work. But even though the man scared her half to death and had obviously dismissed her for the night, she couldn't leave. "Mr. Hogan?"

"Yeah?" He continued to count the till money, not bothering to look at her.

"Would you . . . would ya know of any more part-time jobs around here? Day work? Somethin' I could do before I come here?"

He turned his head and gave her a sharp, keen stare. She trembled inwardly.

"Looty's diner, maybe," he said in his usual terse manner. "But don't be late."

She was already aware that he didn't tolerate tardiness or laziness. That he'd answered her at all thrilled her.

"No, sir. Thank you," she said. "Good night."

He didn't answer.

She opened the door and stepped out into the night, feeling tired and old beyond her years. She hardly noticed the new crisp shift of snow on the ground except to add it to her list of tribulations. Her feet throbbed on the far end of her aching legs as she climbed into the cab of the old pickup truck. She closed her eyes and prayed that the motor would start.

The key to the ignition had disappeared long before Ellis had started driving the old truck, but she knew where all its quirks and idiosyncrasies were to be found. Four pumps on the gas pedal and a quick flick of the ignition turned the motor over in cold weather. Four more pumps and another quick flick, and it usually came to life. However, for Ellis, the truck's best feature was its heater. It worked. Winter and summer.

She waited for the engine to warm up, huddling close inside her coat and wondering how early Looty's diner opened in the morning. She needed to do some laundry too the next day. She drove past the Webster Textiles mill, across the railroad tracks and beyond, to the outskirts of town. She watched for patches of ice on the road and continued with her mental list of things to do as she followed the mountain road to the southeast. An affordable place to live was high priority, along with the second job—a third job might be possible if she could work it in.

She slowed the truck at a familiar bend in the road and turned onto a deserted logging road. About two hundred yards into the woods she stopped. She wasn't sure why she continued to pull off the road. She'd parked the truck in the same place for the past two weeks and had yet to see another vehicle on the old dirt road.

She cracked a side window and left the motor running, storing its heat in the cab as she carefully emptied tip money from her pockets. By the dim overhead light she counted eighteen dollars and thirty-five cents. She sighed heavily. She had a grand total of one hundred ninety-two dollars and eighty-one cents to her name.

Her eyes closed and her head came to rest on the rear window. It was going to take forever to earn the money she needed, she thought wearily. Tired and discouraged, she felt the sting of tears forming in her eyes. She wasn't a quitter and she wasn't a crier. She wouldn't allow her tears to fall.

She leaned forward and reached down behind the seat back that was as loose as a six-year-old's front tooth. She groped for the small paper bag that contained her vast fortune and added her tip money to it.

Her booty was far from the total amount of money she needed to return to Stony Hollow, but, in truth, it was more money than she'd ever seen at one time. Ordinarily, she might have taken some pride in what she'd earned. As it was, she could only wish it were more and endure the ache in her heart.

Her stomach growled as she returned the brown bag to its hiding place and gathered a blanket from the floor of the truck. Under the tattered blanket was a carpet-bag that contained all her worldly possessions, save one. And she missed it horribly.

It was that one small thing that had changed her life from dazed and dependent to discontented and determined five years earlier. The same one that kept her motivated and encouraged when her mind and body wanted to give up and hide. The one her heart clung to as she closed the window, locked both doors, turned off the engine, and covered herself with the blanket. It was the last thing she thought of when she closed her eyes at night and the first that came to mind when she opened them in the morning.

Two

"Anybody in there? Hey. Anybody inside?"

Ellis sat up with a jolt. She'd barely closed her eyes. The voice was a roar in her ears. The rapid pounding on the truck window was nothing compared to the frenzied beat of her heart.

"I got a gun," she shouted at the dark form standing beside the truck. She trembled as if the temperature in the cab had suddenly fallen to sub-zero. "Step away, or I'll blow your head clean off."

Lordy, she wished she *did* have a gun. The presence standing outside the truck door was big and darker than the starless night. Cloud-covered moonlight played tricks with her vision, making it seem as if the human form was there one second, gone the next, and back the next.

"No. Wait. Don't shoot. I mean no harm," came the obviously male voice—belonging to someone who was obviously worried about her nonexistent gun, someone who obviously didn't question the idea that it was as much her God-given right to bear arms as it was to breathe air.

"Who are you? What do you want?" She prayed he couldn't hear the fear in her voice. She hoped she sounded like Granny Yeager back in Stony Hollow.

"I . . . I saw your taillights from the main road. This road ain't used much anymore. I thought you might be in trouble."

"Well, I ain't. Skedaddle."

"Okay. I'm leaving." She narrowed her eyes and peered into the darkness for signs of movement. She couldn't tell if he was leaving or not. She jumped when he spoke again. "Are ya sleepin' out here?"

"That ain't none of your concern, mister. Now git. I don't want to have to shoot ya, but I will if I don't see ya drivin' off before I count to ten. " She grimaced with her lie.

Over the past few years it had become a way of life for her to say things that she knew she couldn't back up. Still, it didn't come naturally. Every time she allowed hollow words to pass across her lips, she'd cringe and pray that no one would test them.

"The reason I'm askin' is . . . well, we got bears in this neck of the woods. Bobcats too. They're pretty hungry this time of year."

Lordy, she hated it when people played her for stupid. There were more bears than people in Stony Hollow, and she was no turnip. She knew bears, and she preferred them to most people.

"One," she began to count.

"It's gonna get colder out here. How are you goin' to stay warm?"

"The heater works. Two."

"You can die from the fumes, ya know."

She hadn't spent the last nineteen years under a rock!

"Three."

"Wait now," he said. "Not everything that goes around in the dark is Santa Claus, ya know."

"Four."

"Stop that countin', for crissake." He sounded flustered but not frightened. "I can't just leave you out here alone. Why don't ya stay in town . . . at McKee's or maybe the boardin' house? I'll go back to town and wake up Jimmy McKee for ya."

"Five."

"Well, at least tell me who you are. I'll need to tell the sheriff when he comes up here to chip ya outta there in the mornin'. Your kin'll want to know how ya died." He paused. "I'm Bryce LaSalle. I live about eight miles up the road back there."

Oh no. Why *him*? she wondered, rolling her eyes heavenward.

"Six."

"I know most everybody in this county and some in the next, but I don't recognize this truck. . . ."

"Seven," she shouted hastily. She could almost hear the bells of realization beginning to chime in his head.

"You're not from around— Ellis? Is that you in there?"

"Eight." Strangers must come to Webster about as often as they come to Stony Hollow, she speculated.

The door of the truck rattled on its hinges when he tried to open it. "Unlock the door, Ellis. It's cold out here."

"Then go home."

"After we talk."

"We got nothin' to say to each other. Go home."

She thought she heard him using cuss words, but when he spoke clear enough for her to understand him, his tone was only mildly threatening.

"If I go home now, I'll call the sheriff and have him come check on you. Want that?"

No, she didn't. There was no way of telling if his threat was as empty as her own, but the last thing she needed was to draw any attention from the law.

She was fully aware of the fact that Bryce had been drinking, and tried to mentally calculate whether the two beers she'd served him could have affected his mind. Taking a big chance, she reached out and popped the lock. The door swung open, and a gust of frigid wind attacked her.

"Put the gun down," Bryce said, fury at having even

an invisible gun aimed at him rippling in his voice. "You don't need it."

"I ain't stupid, mister. I don't hardly know ya, so I'll be keepin' my gun. Speak your piece and be done with it," she said, amazing herself with her own words.

She could hear the limbs of trees cracking from the cold in the silence that followed. Several tense moments passed before he spoke.

"Move over then. It's cold out here."

Oddly enough, she wasn't really afraid of him anymore. His voice was gruff but his manner was easy and benign. She drew her legs up under the blanket and pulled herself across the seat to lean against the far door, making room for him to climb in behind the steering wheel. She felt like a child in a tiny box with a very large authority figure when he slammed the door closed . . . but it didn't last long. She was no little girl anymore.

"What the hell are you doing out here?" he asked point-blank. He couldn't tell if he was more surprised or alarmed to discover her in the woods alone.

"Trying to sleep?" she said, braving impertinence when his attitude stung her pride.

She knew he couldn't see much of her body, much less the expression on her face in the dark. But she felt that he was trying to see her, to study her as he had during much of the evening at the Steel Wheel.

"You have nowhere else to go?" he asked, his voice gentling a bit. "Hasn't Tug paid ya yet?"

"Whether I been paid or not is none of your business," she said, thinking it best to keep quiet about the near fortune under the seat. There was one distinct advantage to being dirt poor—thieves knew they couldn't get blood from a rock and didn't waste their time trying to rob you. "And where I sleep ain't none of your business neither. So why don't ya get out of my truck and go on about what *is* your business."

"You're a sweet talker, ain't ya?" There was a point to

which he would applaud her guts and fortitude, but she'd gone beyond it.

"If it's sweet talkin' ya want, ya got the wrong dog by the tail, mister. I got better things to do. So leave me be."

"You know, I'm of a mind to do just that," he said in a similar tone of voice. "I don't take to thorny women, and I don't mind tellin' ya that I've taken about all the pokin' and jabbin' I'm gonna take from you. Now, I'm trying to be nice here. But I'm beginnin' to think it would be easier to call the sheriff and have him tote ya off to jail for the night."

"You can't do that. I ain't done nothin' wrong, and ya said yourself that nobody ever uses this road."

"You ever heard of vagrancy?"

"I'm no vagrant."

"Then ya do have money?"

"I got a job," she stated, showing a clear knowledge of vagrancy laws.

He fell silent, and she smiled in satisfaction. She crossed her arms over her chest and waited for his next move.

She heard rather than saw him groping about the dash just before the cab light came on, illuminating his handsome features and awaking the squirming critters deep in her abdomen. Lord above! He was the handsomest man! she decided, underscoring the jittery feeling she experienced in his presence.

"You're goin' to drain my battery," she told him, forcing herself to sound calm.

"I'll jump-start ya," he said, pausing when his words conjured up another meaning in his mind. Looking at her more directly, he allowed his gaze to travel and linger where it pleased. She shivered in her blanket as she recognized the light in his eyes. It wasn't exactly the randy expression of lust she was familiar with, but the avid sensuality and desire were undeniable.

Recalling himself, he cleared his throat and added, "I can't talk reason to ya if I can't see you."

"Who asked ya to?"

There was a warning in his frown, but he circumvented her remark and asked, "Where's your gun?"

"I ain't got a gun."

Nodding slowly and considering her thoughtfully, he said nothing. His silence unnerved her.

"I got a knife though. . . ." she said, her tone ominous and quite convincing to her ears.

"Show it to me," he said.

"Make a wrong move and you'll see it soon enough," she said, beginning to feel and sound weak.

He sighed. "What are ya doin' in Webster?"

"Workin'."

"If I promise not to steal your money, will ya tell me if ya have any?"

"No."

He released another long breath and gave her a hard stare.

"Damn, you're as stubborn as a blue-nosed mule. Didn't your mama ever tell ya not to stomp on a helping hand?"

"I never met her, and I don't need no help."

He closed his eyes in a valiant attempt at keeping his temper. Ellis held her breath and was amazed to see him calm and reflective when he finally opened them again.

"Okay. Let's *pretend* that ya have enough money to rent a room in town. Would ya?" he asked.

"No."

"Why not?"

"Why waste the money when I can sleep in my truck?"

He looked away from her. She watched him with a wary eye.

"If you had a million dollars, would ya rent a motel room?" he asked, turning on her abruptly, his words rapid and impatient.

"Sure. If I had a million dollars," she said, surprised by both his outburst and the absurdity of his question.

"So you're not sleeping out here because ya enjoy it."

Her mind focused on the throbbing ache in her back. "'Course not."

"You're savin' your money then. If ya have any, that is."

She chewed on her lower lip, unsure of how to answer the question without giving him any information. She nodded.

"Why the hell didn't ya tell me that to begin with?" he asked.

"Because it wasn't none—"

"—of my business," he said, finishing her most frequently used expression.

Their gazes met, clashed, and they came to an understanding in a split second—then they laughed.

She'd never come across anyone quite like him. His face and the appeal of his body notwithstanding, she had the distinct impression that if he were a fire, she could play with him all she wanted to and never get burned. The idea intrigued her.

"What?" she asked when she looked up to find him staring at her in a peculiar fashion.

"You're real pretty when you smile," he said in a voice that was soft, southern, and seductive.

She looked young and innocent. His eyes narrowed as a thought occurred to him. "You old enough to be workin' at the Wheel?"

"Don't let my baby face fool ya, mister," she said, dismissing her flawless features as a bothersome and irritating impediment in her life. "I'm old enough to do most everthin', 'cept die of old age."

He was still suspicious. "Old enough to drink legally in this state?"

"Almost. But seein' as I don't drink liquor that ain't too important, is it?"

"Tug'll skin ya alive if you're not twenty yet," he warned her. "He's real careful with that liquor license of his."

"We can't have him doin' that, now can we?" she said,

looking out the front window into the darkness when she couldn't force her gaze to meet his honestly.

Eighteen was the legal serving age for beer, to serve anything stronger you had to be twenty, and you had to be twenty-one to drink alcohol in the state of Kentucky. Ellis thought the age distinctions were negligible, not to mention pointless, when a body was in dire need of a job.

Bryce had been digging and probing into her affairs nearly nonstop since his first tap on the truck window. She grew uncomfortable with his silence. A covert glance in his direction told her he was watching her again.

"I got things to do in the mornin', so . . . if you're done stickin' your nose where it don't belong . . ." she said, feeling awkward.

He grinned and laughed. "Are ya askin' me to leave?"

"Yes."

"I thought so," he said, still grinning, his eyes sparkling with humor. With his fingers on the door handle he turned back to her, saying, "I don't suppose you'd take money from me for a room. No strings. You could take your time payin' it back."

"What's this? Charity?" She drew back and stiffened as if he'd spit on her.

He held up both hands. "Sorry. It was just a thought. I knew better than to offer it."

"I don't need charity."

"I know. I'm sorry," he said, shaking his head. He'd made a stupid move and he knew it. She had too much pride to take even the smallest kindness from him, but he couldn't reconcile himself to leaving her cold, alone, and unprotected.

"That thing with the gun was good. Had me shakin' in my boots," he said, stalling.

"Really?" She thought of Granny Yeager and was flattered by his compliment. Praise wasn't something she was used to, but she thought she could learn to like it.

"Really. But the knife couldn't split a biscuit and butter it." She thought it best not to comment.

After one long final inspection of her, he said, "Good night, Ellis."

Ellis leaned her head against the rear window of the truck and listened to the fading crunch, crunch, crunch of Bryce's footsteps in the frozen snow outside. She smiled. She fancied Bryce LaSalle more than any man she'd ever met before. He was big and strong and handsome, but what she especially admired was that he laughed and listened and didn't fly off the handle when he was angry or frustrated.

She favored the way he made her feel too—safe and worth worrying about. New feelings that she wanted to embrace but approached with caution.

"Steady, Ellis," she said aloud, reestablishing her priorities and putting Bryce on the bottom of the pile. She didn't have time to fill her head with sparkling cobwebs and fairy tales. She had responsibilities. She had promises to keep. She had plans for her life, and none of them included Bryce LaSalle.

She scooted back behind the steering wheel and performed the little song and dance that started the engine to warm the cab again. She opened the window a smidgen and smiled as she relaxed to await the heat.

He surely made her feel funny, she thought, her mind slipping back to Bryce involuntarily. She stroked her abdomen mindlessly as she recalled the airy flutters and pulsating sensations that his presence stirred. The breathlessness. The erratic beating of her heart. She wondered if these queer spells were the feelings she'd heard other women speak of from time to time.

Effie Watson had once told her that sometimes there was a commotion in a woman's body that told her to mate with a certain man, and that once felt, the urge could build to be so great that it would drive a woman plum insane. More than once, Effie had laid the blame for Ellis's birth on that very urge. Was what she felt with Bryce the commotion Effie had told her about? The thought concerned her deeply. She knew what came from mating with a man—babies. And at the moment, a baby wasn't what she'd call a *better* alternative to going insane.

"Ellis?"

"Ayah!" she cried, startled by a loud thump on the window beside her. Again she saw the blacker than black silhouette of a man outside the truck.

"It's just me," Bryce bellowed over the clamor of the engine.

"You're wearin' on my nerves," she said sharply, rolling the window down a little more.

"Scared?" She couldn't see his face but she heard the teasing grin in his voice.

"No. I was . . . thinkin'. What do you want now?"

"I waited to see if you were gonna need that jump-start on your motor, but then I got to thinkin' . . ." She groaned, and her head fell against the window with a thud. "Listen now. I think I can help you." She groaned again. "Okay. Forget it."

Over the unsteady roar of the engine she could hear him walking away. Her curiosity got the better of her.

"Wait," she called, opening the door but not getting out. "I got the awfullest feelin' I shouldn't ask, but what were ya thinkin' about?"

Crunch, crunch, crunch.

"You," he said, closer to her than she'd realized. Her hand pressed against the riot in her belly. "I was thinkin' about you."

"Well, don't." Lord, that was all she needed. She'd go insane for sure. "Forget ya ever met me, will ya? I don't want ya thinkin' about me."

"Can't help it. You're on my mind."

Ellis wanted to scream. If she threw him in a river, the man would float upstream!

"Tell me what ya gotta say. I'm lettin' all my heat out here."

"I was wonderin' if you'd consider takin' a second job? It ain't permanent work, only part-time for a couple months. It doesn't pay much, but it comes with a room and meals," he said.

"What is it? What do I have to do?" she asked, a master of distrust.

"Cooking. Cleaning. Nothing much, really. My sister-in-law is expectin' her baby soon. She works at the mill all day, and she gets real tired. Her and my brother have been talkin' about gettin' someone to come in to help out for a while," he said casually, though he was far from feeling it. He felt a tremendous need to get the little angel in out of the cold and protect her, as if it were a religious crusade. He wasn't sure why, only that he did.

"They was plannin' to get live-in help?" she asked. Were they rich?

"Well, no," he admitted, readily adding, "But if you were willin' to take a small cut in pay to help with the food, they could put ya up. The house is big and ya met my brother—he's a good ol' boy—and Anne, his wife, is the best." He paused. "She'd be grateful for the help," he said in a soft, persuasive voice when she continued to hold back her enthusiasm.

Pregnant, huh? No woman that Ellis had ever known got help *before* the baby was born.

"If she's poorly, how come she's still workin' at the mill?" she asked, sensing there was something cock-eyed in Bryce's offer.

"Who? Anne? She's as healthy as a horse, 'cept she's tired all the time."

"Well, if she's on her feet, there's no call for—"

"Buck's nuts about her," he said, breaking in as he tucked his hands in his armpits to keep them warm. She could hear him flapping his arms like a chicken to keep his blood moving in the cold. "And he's a little . . . excited about this baby. I think he'd stay home and wait on her hand and foot himself, if he didn't have to pay the doctor bills."

What a strange notion. Ellis thought she might take the job, just to watch Buck. However, as amused as she was, she was also thinking with the practical side of her brain. Winter was only beginning, and the weather held no promise of getting any warmer for several months to come. Living in a house would be safer, she knew. She couldn't fulfill her promise or get back what belonged to her if she were sick or hurt or worse. Besides, how much trouble could it be to clean up after two people who weren't home most of the day?

"I'll do what I can to help this sister-in-law of yours, but I can't see that it'd be all that much," she said.

"You can work that out with her in the m-morning," he said, wondering when he'd get a chance to discuss his plan with Buck and Anne. His teeth chattered while the truck's heater blew hot air up inside Ellis's blanket. "Follow me. It ain't far."

"I'm not goin' with ya tonight," she said, appalled at the suggestion.

"Why not?" Ah, jeez. Couldn't she be beautiful and magnificently independent and proud without being stubborn?

"Don't ya know what time it is? They'll be fast asleep."

"Th-that's okay. I can sh-show ya your room and you c-can meet them in the m-m-mornin'."

"What if they don't like me? What if she's got someone else in mind for the job?"

"They don't, and they'll l-like ya fine." Damn, it was cold. He couldn't feel his toes anymore.

"You don't know that. And ya don't sleep in some-body's house without their permission and then ask 'em for a job in the mornin'. Even hillbillies know things ain't done like that."

"They won't mind ya s-sleepin' there. They know how c-cold it is out here, even if you d-don't. Fact is, it's still part my house t-too, so I can invite ya to st-stay."

"You live there too?" Uh-oh. She hadn't thought about being under the same roof with *him*. Panic and delight wrestled in her midsection. Would goin' insane be as painful as birthin' a baby? she wondered.

"I don't have to live there," he said, picking up on her

hesitation. Hell, he'd move to another state if he could only get the two of them in out of the cold before they both froze to death.

"What?"

"There's another house. I c-can move in there. I only moved back into the b-big house for the winter anyway."

"I don't know . . ." she hedged, not wanting to put him out of his own house and not wanting to be in constant battle with her emotions at the same time.

"You've made up your m-mind about not comin' tonight, haven't ya?"

"Yes."

"Then come in the mornin'. Meet Anne. Ch-check out the house and m-make up your mind then. Okay?" He was shivering and eager to have some sort of an affirmative answer from her. Just one yes from her, and he could die a happy man.

"Okay."

"Great." He muttered something under his breath and cursed the weather. "I'm freezin' my . . . I'm freezin' to death. Lock your doors. I'll come b-back for ya first thing in the mornin'," he said, and then he was gone.

Three

Ellis woke at first light, stiff and cold and just as bone weary as she had been the night before. There wasn't room enough in the cab of the truck to cuss a cat without getting fur in her teeth—let alone get a good night's rest. Yet parts of her were feeling enthusiastic, her mind lingering in a recurrent dream of being cared about and belonging, her senses anticipating Bryce's arrival.

By the time the engine had produced enough heat to eliminate the chill in her bones, she had scurried out of the truck for a plastic bowl full of snow, waited for it to melt, and quickly washed herself. She changed into clean clothes and began to brush out the thick, straight, blond hair that hung to below her shoulders.

Sleeping in a safe warm bed that was big enough to stretch out on had taken on a new importance during the night, and she wanted all the LaSalles to like her. . . . Well, at least that was her conscious reasoning for taking extra care with her hair and pinching roses into her pale cheeks.

That she was lonely and starving for the smallest crumb of human fellowship she would deny with her dying breath. People were mean and hurtful, she reminded herself, and she didn't need them. She determined that she'd move out of the LaSalles' place the second she could afford to.

Nope, she didn't need anybody, she told herself. Moments of insecurity, fear, and loneliness were simply regressions to another time in her life. Food and a bed were all she wanted from the LaSalles. And she would earn them fairly. The fidgets she felt in her abdomen came from the wanting, that's all.

She laced her fingers in her lap and sat quietly watching the woods come to life as she pondered the events of the night before. Had they really happened? Or had they been another one of her silly dreams?

Looking through the window at the large footprints in the snow was somehow reassuring, but they brought back memories of a little girl who was full of hope and love and faith in the people who made up her world. She called to mind how the faith had been strangled to death, the love neglected and ignored to wither and blow away in the harsh winds of life. Hope had remained many years longer, to be beaten and bruised at every opportunity until she came to know that the only hope she had was her own will to survive.

The sun had barely cleared the mountaintops before she had convinced herself that Bryce wasn't coming for her, and to have put so much stock in the soft words of a stranger had been foolish.

As reluctantly as one would throw away something dear but irreparably damaged, she set Bryce and his job offer firmly out of her mind. If she was going to try to get a job at Looty's diner, it would be best to get there early, before it opened for breakfast.

With no room on the logging road to turn around, she backed the truck onto the main road and was heading toward town when a green and white four-wheeler drove up behind her, horn blaring.

She recognized the driver seconds before he passed her on the road, slowing as he moved in front of her and eventually forcing her to a stop. She felt a nervous anticipation as she sat in her truck.

In Ellis's opinion, Bryce had a unique way of reacting and responding to things. Amusement, however, was still the last thing she'd expected to see in his face when he got out of his truck and walked back to hers. He was a very strange man indeed.

"Did ya change your mind about the job?" he asked after she rolled the window down. "Or did ya decide that I couldn't be trusted?" He already knew the answer.

"Why should I trust ya?" she asked, honest whenever possible.

"'Cuz I haven't done anything to make ya *not* trust me, have I?" he asked, his voice hoarse and raspy.

Well . . . no, he hadn't, but she hadn't known him twenty-four hours yet. . . .

He was going to have to step up his pace if he was going to keep up with and eventually catch this little gal, he decided, admiring her pluck once again. And catch her was exactly what he intended to do. He'd been awake all night thinking about her. She'd caused him to catch a cold, and frustrated and fascinated him more than any women he'd known before. She deserved to be caught.

He chuckled and shook his head at her. "What about the job? I talked to Anne, and she's willing to look ya over."

"I suppose ya told her all about me." It rankled what little vanity she had to think of him describing her as the poor hillbilly girl who worked at the Steel Wheel and slept in a beat-up truck.

"How could I do that? I don't know all about ya." He paused, then added, "Yet," making it sound as if it were a temporary inconvenience. He regarded her with a steady gaze. His smile was that of an interrogator who knew ways of getting her to talk. Her heart lurched anxiously.

She scowled at him. "Are ya taking me to see your sister-in-law or not?"

"Yes, ma'am." He covered his mouth and coughed

harshly several times, then added, "There's a turn-around down the road a piece."

They wriggled and wrangled their way along the mountainside to a dirt road that led to a house as big as Mr. Johnson's back in Stony Hollow. A two-story house with a broad wraparound front porch, it was freshly painted and well kept. The pale yellow house with dark green trim was distinctively cheerful and bright. It was homey looking with the snow on the ground and the tall, drab trees of winter slumbering all about it.

Ellis parked the truck beside Bryce's at the bottom of a low incline in front of the house. A brisk wind tore at her face and hair when she opened the door and jumped to the ground. She pulled her too-large wool coat close to her and battled the currents of air to join him on the stone path that led to the house. He was coughing again when she got to him.

"No need to be nervous," he told her, inspecting her with a keen eye. "You'll like Anne."

"I ain't nervous," she lied without flinching. "Worse they can say is no, then I can get to Looty's sooner than I thought to."

"You got a date?" he asked, taken back.

"A what?"

"A date? You meetin' someone at Looty's for break-fast?" he asked. The thought that she might be inter-ested in someone else hadn't entered his mind, but it would explain why he felt there was a ten-foot pole between them. "I mean . . . 'cuz if you are, we can do this later. . . ."

"I ain't goin' for breakfast." She hadn't eaten a morn-ing meal since she'd left Stony Hollow. "I'm goin' for a job."

"Another job? Besides this one and the one at the Wheel?"

"If I can puzzle 'em together."

He studied her with a thoughtful frown.

"Are you in trouble?" he asked.

She sensed more of an offer to help than an accusation in his words and demeanor, but it didn't stop the panic that rose up within her, or the defensive shield that automatically fell into place.

"'Course I ain't in trouble," she said, scowling indignantly to convince him. "Why would ya ask such a thing?"

He coughed into his fist, shook his head, then gave her a sheepish grin. "I don't know. Just a feelin' I been gettin'."

"Why?" What was she doing wrong? she wondered.

"I don't know." He shrugged uneasily, searching for words to explain himself. With all the thinking he'd been doing about her, it seemed he'd skipped over a couple of heavy-duty issues, he noted. Such as a boyfriend. And her strange behavior. It was amazin' what a pretty face could do to a man. "You don't talk much. Ya ain't friendly. You're lookin' to take every job in the county. I . . . ya got money but ya won't use it to keep yourself from freezin' to death. Seems to me that's all a might strange for a woman your age."

"Well, if it ain't chickens, it's feathers," she muttered smartly as she turned and stomped up the path ahead of him. "I don't talk 'cuz I ain't got nothin' to say. I ain't friendly 'cuz I ain't got any friends here. I work 'cuz I need the money. And I need the money 'cuz I got plans for my life." She spun around to face him. "What is so almighty strange about that? For any woman any age?"

Stunned, he stood and stared at her open-mouthed for a few seconds before his eyes began to twinkle with a private humor and he chuckled. "Buck'll probably move out, but Anne is gonna *love* you," he said, a certain admiration in his expression. "And I'm real sorry if I hurt your feelin's, Ellis. I didn't set out to."

Well, if he wasn't the beatin'est man she'd ever met. She marveled. Imagine him apologizing to her!

"Pay it no mind," she mumbled, looking away awkwardly, unsure of how to handle the new experience. He coughed again. "You comin' down with somethin'?"

"Just a little cough. Tell me about these dreams you

got for your life," he said affably, nudging her arm gently with his hand as he started toward the house once more.

"They ain't dreams, they're plans. There's a difference."

"Okay. Tell me about these plans of yours." He was trying hard to be congenial, but, Lord, she was a cantankerous female.

"They ain't none of your concern," she stated, drawing a startled look from him. Feeling she owed him for the apology, she added in a softer voice, "They ain't no one's concern but my own."

He studied her intently, and for the second time in as many minutes, he amazed her with a mild reaction. He simply nodded and said, "All right. Let's hurry this along, then, so you can get down to Looty's. I feel like I'm holdin' up progress."

Instead of knocking he entered the house shouting, "Anne? Buck?" The strain brought on another coughing episode that lasted long enough to plow a furrow of concern in Ellis's brow. When he could catch his breath, he pointed toward the back of the house with his thumb, saying, "Water. I'll be back directly."

She excused him with a nod of her head and turned her attention to the interior of the house. She'd seen pictures in magazines of elegant houses with fancy furnishings; she'd lived in a shack with rough pine fittings and a dirt floor; but she'd never seen anything that looked more like a home to her.

The heavy overstuffed furniture with the bright pillows, the polished tables and shiny floors, the rag rug in the center of the main room, and the fire crackling cheerfully in the hearth pulled at her heart. Envy stormed within her. Not for the house or the material possessions inside it—the LaSalles weren't exactly what she'd call stiff in the heels, or eatin' long corn. They weren't rich. But it was too plain to see the wealth of love, care, and pride that they'd poured into making their house a home, a stable and peaceful place. They had what Ellis wanted—something she'd never had. Begrudging the LaSalles their great fortune wasn't in her, but, still, she couldn't help wishing . . .

Footsteps from the second floor caught her attention, and she watched a pregnant woman slowly descend the stairs. A skilled eye judged her to be in her sixth or seventh month and as healthy as the horse Bryce had spoken of. Half-way down she caught sight of Ellis and smiled.

"You have to be Ellis," Anne LaSalle said, her striking blue eyes bright and welcoming. "Bryce said you'd be the prettiest little thing I've seen in a month of Sundays."

Ellis almost turned to see if someone was standing behind her. Bryce thought *she* was pretty?

"With no response forthcoming, Anne continued to speak. "I'm Anne LaSalle, and I've very pleased to meet you, Ellis," she said, holding her hand out in friendship. They touched briefly, measuring and assessing each other in a split second.

Anne met Ellis's gaze openly and equally. There was no pity, prejudice, or condescension. There was no air of employer inspecting employee or of a married woman examining a female intruder in her home. There was only Anne and Ellis, two female human beings standing two feet apart at a crossroad. What was behind them was behind them, and they could choose to take separate roads and go on about their lives or travel together on the same road as friends.

They intuitively chose friendship.

"Mornin', ma'am," Ellis said by way of a greeting.

"Oh, not another one," Anne cried in mock despair. "Every time I think I'm free of that title, I run into another southerner who calls me *ma'am*." She laughed. "Please call me Anne. *Ma'am* makes me feel as old as these hills." She paused. "Of course, now that I look like one of them . . ." She looked down at her belly.

Ellis smiled. "After the babe comes, you'll miss havin' it so close to ya."

Anne palmed her distended abdomen fondly and gave some consideration to her words. She looked almost sad for a moment. "I shouldn't be so impatient, should I?"

"No, ma'am . . . No, you shouldn't." She noticed that Anne was looking at her thoughtfully. Hastily she added, "But it seems like all the mamas I ever met didn't know about the missin' feelin' till after the first one come, either. They was all hankerin' to be done with it too."

"Well, it's just one of the many things I don't know about having babies. I haven't even held a newborn before."

"Some of it comes to ya natural, and the rest ya learn real quick. Little ones are tougher than they look and just sorta live in spite of ya," she said, trying to be reassuring, a pang of guilt tearing at her.

Anne laughed. "That's good to know. Have you had breakfast yet, Ellis? I'm starved."

"You're always starved," came Buck's voice from the stairway several feet away. "A camp of lumberjacks could live for a week on what you eat in one sittin', sugar." He stepped to his wife's side and planted a kiss on her cheek. "Hey, Ellis. Mighty glad to have ya with us."

"Glad to be here," she said.

"We gotta talk fast to keep her though," Bryce said, coming up behind his brother and sister-in-law. "She's lookin' to hire on at Looty's too."

"Well, let's move away from the front door and talk about it over breakfast, shall we?" Anne suggested politely.

"Annie's starvin' again," Buck said, interpreting her remark for Bryce, who chuckled.

"We gotta feed her then. Last time she missed a meal she started gnawin' on the furniture."

Anne sniffed and gave them both a haughty glare. She reached out and looped her arm with Ellis's, saying, "Do you see what I have to put up with around here, Ellis? Please say you'll come and stay with us for a while. I'm in dire need of help."

She found herself being pulled toward the kitchen and wasn't at all sure of what to say. She'd never seen such goin's-on. Them sassin' one another and sayin' the most outrageous things. It was the beatin'est thing.

"What kind of help were ya needin'?" she asked in all seriousness.

Anne was quick to pick up on Ellis's tension. It wasn't the first time she'd been made aware of the fact that men like the LaSalle brothers were few and far between and that she was one lucky woman to have fallen in love with a man who wasn't afraid to treat her as an equal.

"Actually, I need someone to help out a little with the house and the cooking. Do you cook?" she asked.

"'Course." Didn't every female over the age of seven? she thought.

"Anne was a Yankee before she married Buck," Bryce said simply.

Bryce's candid explanation shed a great deal of light on the situation for Ellis. Though the war between the states had come to an end over a hundred years earlier, it was common knowledge in the South that circumstance alone had kept the better army from winning.

"Oh," she said, wiser but not thinking any less of Anne as a person. "Well, I reckon I can do most anything that needs doin' if ya tell me what ya want. I ain't up on my book learnin', but I can cook and mend and clean and plow—'course you won't be needin' that done till spring, but I can chop wood and—"

"Oh my," Anne said, holding up a hand to stop her, laughing. "You're going to make me look bad if you don't stop. You wouldn't believe the time I had getting Buck to marry me when he found out I couldn't chop wood or plow a field. Please don't remind him of what a terrible bargain he made on me."

Ellis opened her mouth to deny that she'd ever dream of doing such a thing, but Anne winked at her and grinned. Buck and Bryce were chuckling, too, she noticed, which added to her confusion. They were the strangest people she'd ever met, and they fascinated her.

It was hard to tell what they spoke of in earnest and what they were funning about, but underneath all the words and theatrical facial expressions there was a current of caring and understanding, a prevailing relationship between the three of them that was close and loving—and she was in total awe of it.

Under Anne's direction, she helped prepare breakfast while the two of them discussed what would be expected of her in return for room and board. Mention was made of a small salary for her services, but she refused it. The bottom line in the deal revealed that there was very little that needed doing. In all honesty, she ought to be giving *them* money for putting a roof over her head. Luckily, she wasn't foolish enough to be that honest.

The four of them sat together over the meal, something not unheard of in Stony Hollow, but a custom she was unacquainted and uncomfortable with.

She liked listening to Anne speak with her proper northern accent. She said *isn't* and *not*, instead of *ain't*, the way it was written in the books that had belonged to Ellis's mother. She didn't drop her *g*'s the way the rest of them did, and she didn't end every other word with an *uh* sound. It was nice, sort of fresh and crisp and clean sounding.

When everyone had finished eating, Ellis stood and began to clear away the dishes.

"I'll do these," Bryce said, standing with his plate and reaching for Anne's. Ellis froze like a statue, staring at him. "Stop gawkin'," he said, a little defensive. "It's my turn."

"He and Buck took turns doing the dishes and the rest of the chores for years before I arrived on the scene," Anne explained with tongue in cheek. "Who was I to march in and change everything?"

Both men groaned as if they had a mouthful of bad moonshine.

"Is that the way you remember it?" Buck asked Bryce, handing over his plate with a befuddled expression.

"Nope. Seems to me like she marched in and changed everything *except* takin' turns at the chores."

Buck's gaze was loving and filled with laughter as it came to rest on Anne. "Remember the day she told us that she was my wife and not some fancy maid?"

"Like yesterday," he mumbled, turning toward the sink.

"And that if she was goin' to work full time at the mill alongside us, then we could just keep on doin' the housework alongside her." Anne smiled serenely but did not comment.

"She don't chop wood though," Bryce reminded him, humor twitching at the corners of his lips when his eyes made contact with Ellis's. He was being playful, as if he didn't care a whit whether Anne could chop wood or not.

"Well, I can't give birth to a baby, so I reckon we're pretty well matched there," Buck said, then added, "'Course, I'd feel better about keepin' her, and I could hold my head up down at the Wheel again if she'd just go barefoot and learn to plow fields."

Anne was very northern and very big city, so it was a comic thought to the LaSalles, who laughed heartily until they noticed Ellis.

"Are ya makin' game of me?" she asked, soft voiced, stiff necked, and uncertain. The ribbing hadn't been aimed directly at her, but she felt mocked just the same. She was ready to cry from the hurt and spit in their faces with pride at the same time.

"No. Oh no. No," they answered at once, looking mortified and guilty of being insensitive. A short tense silence followed the disclaimer as the LaSalles frantically sought words to explain themselves and put Ellis at ease again.

Bryce spoke first.

"You gotta lighten up, Ellis," he said, not ungently as he pried the plate from her hands and took her coffee cup from the table, going on about his business. "We pull Anne's chain every chance we get to keep her head from swellin' up like a hot-air balloon. See, about eighteen months ago she saved Webster from becomin' another ghost town in these parts, and there ain't a soul in the whole damn town—includin' Buck and me—who don't think she's the best thing that's happened to the world since safety pins and sliced bread."

"And ball-point pens and flip-top cans," Buck added, winking at his wife.

"Don't forget Velcro, sweetheart," she said, grinning before she lowered her eyes in what looked to Ellis like embarrassment.

Bryce picked up Ellis's coat on his way back to the table and was holding it out for her as he continued. "We tease her 'cuz it's our way of tellin' her we care about her. It didn't have nothin' to do with you."

She slid her arms into the big woolen coat feeling humbled and in the wrong. Confused too. Was she being handed her coat and asked to leave because she hadn't understood their banter? Because she was more used to ridicule than tomfoolery? She hadn't meant to make them feel uncomfortable, but she wouldn't abide anyone throwing off on her if she didn't have to. Should she apologize or not? She had a feeling that she'd just kissed her warm, safe bed good-bye.

"Saturdays are busy for Looty," Bryce was saying. "You'd best get a move on. You can do your unpackin' when ya get back."

She turned to look at him. There was nothing in his expression that implied anger. He nodded and gave her an encouraging smile.

"Good luck, Ellis," Anne said. Both she and Buck were looking on with kind faces and friendly smiles, perplexing her all the more.

She nodded her thanks, feeling she ought to do

something to repay their generosity. She looked around at the messy kitchen.

"No, now," Anne said, laboring to her feet. "Don't look at Bryce's dishes like that, or he'll have you doing his chores and I'll never get him whipped back into shape after the baby comes. You run along and get that job at Looty's, and when you come home, you and I'll sit down and make a list of all the things I can't bend over to do anymore."

She silently expressed her understanding and turned to leave, then turned back.

"Thank you for the meal," she said. "And I'm sorry I made a fuss before."

She beat it out of the house and sighed with relief in the frigid morning air. She jumped when she heard Bryce coughing behind her.

"Are ya all right?" he asked when he could.

It was on the tip of her tongue to tell him that she was just fine, but she wasn't, and different words came forward.

"I made a fool of myself," she said, dismayed.

He didn't deny it or try to offer words of sympathy, and she couldn't seem to stop more words from coming forth.

"They're very strange," she said, in case he hadn't noticed. "Them teasin' and flirtin' like they're courtin'. And none of ya get mad like you're supposed to."

He chuckled. "Would ya feel better if we did?"

She thought about it. She was conditioned to anger, but she didn't enjoy it. On the other hand, she knew how to deal with anger, and kindness made her feel . . . queer.

"Maybe I would," she said.

He laughed again. He slipped his hands into the bends of his arms to keep them warm and stepped off the porch to the stone path beside her.

"Well, first off, ya ain't done nothing for us to get mad about, and secondly, you'll get used to us. Though I'll warn ya," he said, motioning back to the house with his head, "they get a lot worse than what ya saw this mornin'. They're crazy in love and they kiss and hug till it makes ya wanna throw up, but ya get used to that, too, after a while. . . ."

"You're humbuggin' me again, ain't ya?" she accused him.

"Yeah." He grinned and she trembled, but not from the cold. His arms unfolded and slipped loosely about her waist. "We do that when we like someone."

Did that mean he liked her? Well, of course he must like her, or he wouldn't be helping her, but . . . in what way did he like her? How much or how little? He *was* standing awfully close to her, she noticed, her muscles tensing, her nerves in a state of chaos, her heart racing.

"What do you do when ya like someone, Ellis?" he asked, his voice as soft as goose down. He sensed her discomfort at being touched. She wasn't repulsed or he'd have sensed that, too, and withdrawn his hands. It was more as if she wasn't used to being touched, and it puzzled him.

Her eyes lowered slowly away from his while she thought about his question. There weren't so many people in her life that she'd noticed a great distinction in her behavior toward them. There were those she'd loved without reservation, those she'd tolerated or endured . . . but liked?

Ellis liked to see the sun dancing on water, and she liked the smell of spring after a heavy rain. She liked the way babies laughed and the taste of honeysuckle. She liked hot Sunday afternoons and . . . she liked Bryce, she admitted with some difficulty. It wasn't something she'd had occasion to acknowledge about another human being before.

She did like Bryce. She liked his sense of self, his confidence, and his easy manner. She liked his common sense, his obvious devotion to his family and friends, his willingness to help a stranger in need. She liked the control he had on his emotions, his patience, and his persistent attempts to understand her.

"You best get back inside," she muttered when his cough broke into her thoughts.

He wasn't inclined to argue, nor was he going to press her for an answer to his question. It was no revelation to him that personal disclosures weren't something that came easily to her. He wished her well at Looty's, planted a quick good-luck kiss on her lips because he couldn't resist the impulse, then took the steps two at a time back to the porch.

"Thank you," she said, her lips steaming, her cheeks flushed.

"For what?" he asked, turning to look at her.

"For . . . for carin'."

His smile was slow and small, but it was the sweetest, gentlest smile she'd ever seen.

"My pleasure."

Four

Looty Miller was sixty years old and as busy as a bee on a watermelon rind.

"Are ya sickly?" the pursy woman asked. Her stout body brushed past Ellis, wafting the odor of grease and onions behind her as she poured coffee into two mugs and set them in front of two men sitting at the counter.

"No ma'am," Ellis said, watching the woman's hands. They seemed to fly with speed and accuracy as they set napkins and spoons beside the mugs and pushed the cream and sugar closer.

"Do ya read and write?" The woman went to the grill and turned bacon strips and eggs with one hand and put bread in a toaster with the other.

"A little."

"Try this," she said, thrusting a menu in Ellis's hand.

"Welcome to Looty's . . ." she read slowly.

"Lower."

"Breakfast. One egg, bacon or sausage, grits or hash browns, toast or biscuits. One dollar, seventy-five. Two eggs, bacon or—"

"When can ya start?"

"Right now?"

"Grab that there apron then," Looty said, serving two customers their breakfast. "I've had my husband's niece aworkin' in here for two years now, and she never comes on time and she forgets to call when she ain't comin' in at all. I been waitin' for a good excuse ta get rid of her, but I reckon most folks thought not to ask for a job here, thinking I'd keep her on just 'cuz she's kin. What'd you say your name was?"

"Ellis, ma'am."

"Well, Ellis, I got news for my husband's niece. She ain't no kin to me, and I'm tired of not bein' able to count on her. Ya picked a good day ta come lookin' for work, girl. Take that half of the place," she motioned to the entire right side of the diner, "and if ya get into trouble, holler."

"Yes, ma'am."

Soon there were two bees buzzin' and busy at Looty's. Ellis took orders at the tables and booths on the right side of the front door and up and down the counter, and Looty did the cooking and took orders left of the door. She also managed the till after Ellis called for help during her first attempt at it.

The breakfast rush lasted another hour before it began to slack off. Looty took time to show her the cash register and to explain the ins and outs of her business. She did a week's work on Saturday as most everyone in the county chose that day to come to town to shop and do business, and the mill ran on half-crews to cut the overhead, freeing more mill workers to be out and about as well. Sunday morning the rush came closer to midmorning, with folks stopping by after church services. Friday and Saturday nights varied, depending on the movie being shown at the theater, firehall dances, and activities at the high school. The rest of the time her customers consisted of a few regulars who came in at distinct intervals during the day and kept Looty busy enough to need somebody to help her.

"I need to tell ya that I got another part-time job," Ellis told Looty, wanting there to be no misunderstandings between them. "Two, actually. Mr. Hogan hired me to work at the Steel Wheel noon to six every day 'cept

Sunday, and Friday and Saturday nights if one of his regular girls don't show up."

With social hours being similar in both the bar and the diner, Ellis's working hours didn't sit too well with Looty, but before she made any judgment, she said, "You said two other jobs."

"I'm helpin' out at the LaSalles. Buck and Anne LaSalle?"

"Know 'em well," she said. "You helpin' till the baby comes?"

"Yes, ma'am. And I ain't sure what all I'll be doin' yet or how much time I'll be needin' to do it, but I'm gettin' meals and a bed, so . . ."

"How bad you want this job, girl?" she asked, her eyes narrowing keenly as she studied Ellis.

"Bad, ma'am."

The old woman continued to stare and consider.

"I open here at six sharp every mornin'. You come when you're finished at the LaSalle's place, but no later than eight. I'll keep ya till 'leven-thirty, then you can go on down the road to Tug's place," Looty said, taking over Ellis's life the way she had the conversation. "You'll be wantin' some time off, so Sunday's ya stay half the day."

"No, ma'am. I mean, I wouldn't mind workin' the whole day. I . . . I need the extra money."

"You'll need the time to rest your body more," the older woman said firmly. "Sunday's are half-days, and iffen I can't handle the rest, I'll have to give that no-good niece of my husband's a second chance. Between whiles, we'll watch how ya do here, and if ya work out, we'll follow the money you're makin' at both places. Ya might have your druthers and take a mind to workin' more here and less there."

"Yes ma'am," she said, the proud owner of three jobs. Her spirit traveled miles over the tree-covered mountaintops to Stony Hollow. It hovered over a small shack with a stone chimney, listening to those within. It grew warm and content and hopeful of joining them soon.

She waited on tables at Looty's till half past eleven, then went directly to the Steel Wheel to do the same, paying little attention to the noon hour as it came and went, less to the meal she missed. If the truth be known, her breakfast at the LaSalles had been the hardiest meal she'd had in two weeks. She hardly noticed the twinges of hunger anymore.

By early evening, her pockets weren't exactly bulging with tip money, but they were twice as heavy as the night before. Her feet felt the same. Twice as heavy and throbbing twice as hard. The ache in her calves and lower back reminded her of a night with little sleep in cramped quarters, and she smiled, thinking of the bed awaiting her at the LaSalle house.

"I don't suppose you're smilin' like that 'cuz you're thinkin' of me," said a familiar voice at her side.

She turned and leaned her elbow on the bar as if he hadn't startled her, as if she'd been expecting to see him, as if her knees hadn't suddenly gone weak, but she didn't speak. She pretended to watch Tug Hogan fill her tray with beer bottles as Bryce's clean, soapy scent filled her senses. She swallowed hard, her heart fluttering wildly in her chest.

"Were ya thinkin' about how dashin' and charmin' I am?" said Bryce, teasing her with his eyes.

"Ya think so much of yourself, I ain't about to waste my time on it," she said, raising her voice above the music from the jukebox.

"Auk!" he cried, throwing his hands over his heart and looking to the bartender for help, "Am I bleedin', Tug? This here's my favorite shirt." He looked back at Ellis. "You ever met such a prickly gal before?"

"Hadn't noticed she was, till you come in," he said, surprise registering in the slight elevation of his bushy brows.

"Trust me," Bryce said, rubbing his wound. "Can ya believe that she's not thinkin' me a dashin' and charmin' fellah, after all I've done to convince her that I am? What's a fellah gotta do to get her attention?" he asked the bar owner, grinning playfully.

Tug glanced at Ellis, who was feeling much too warm, then back to Bryce. "Try orderin' a beer."

Bryce's laughter dissolved into a cough. It was several seconds before he could chuckle and speak again. "That's real original thinkin' for a bartender, Tug. A fine idea." Ellis turned away to deliver the beers on her tray. "Any other suggestions?" she heard him ask.

She bit her lower lip as she weaved between tables, over outstretched legs and around chairs. Had Bryce really come to see her? she wondered, or had he come in to drink? Did he truly want her attention, or was he teasin' her again, playin' and flirtin' with her in the manner that came so natural to him?

She hadn't forgotten Liddy Evans, either. She didn't hold with one woman taking up with another woman's man. Bryce's relationship with another man's woman was his business—though it somehow seemed less sinful when she thought of Liddy's husband.

Bryce fell into conversation with Tug and didn't speak to her again, yet she was acutely conscious of his gaze. She came and went from the bar with her orders, feeling as nervous as a long-tailed cat in a room full of rocking chairs.

Time crawled by. She kept hoping he'd leave without speaking to her—still she was expecting him to say something and found herself feeling disappointed when he didn't. Her emotions grated back and forth on her nerves like a saw.

His arm would brush against her shoulder, or he'd turn on his stool to look at her and graze her hip with his knee, and she'd step away as if burnt. She was unsteady, ready to topple.

"Racks are gettin' low," Tug said, setting four beer bottles and a glass on her tray. "Stock 'em when ya can."

"Yes, sir." She delivered the beers and the specially ordered glass and went straight to the cooler. She took bottles out of boxes four at a time, two in each hand, and set them on the shelves separating the bar from the cooler. The task was nearly finished before she caught Bryce watching her through the glass doors on the other side.

"I'd take it kindly if you'd stop watchin' me," she muttered through one side of her mouth a few minutes later, being careful not to look at him directly. She leaned her back against the bar and rubbed warmth into her arms.

"How can ya tell I been watchin' ya?" he asked, leaning close to be heard over the din in the bar.

"I seen ya."

"So that means . . . you've been watchin' *me*," he said, pleased with his own insightfulness. "Quite a coincidence, don't ya think?"

She gasped, and the truth burned in her cheeks. Intending to give him an indignant tongue-lashing, she turned to see his teasing grin and the frolicsome gleam in his eyes. She snapped her mouth closed and looked away, not knowing how to respond.

"Ah, Ellis," he said, laughing softly. "You don't have much of a sense of humor, do ya? You're just not sure what to make of me, are ya?"

She looked at him and decided to be honest. "You're the beatin'est thing I ever come across."

"How so?"

In so many ways she was hard put to find a place to begin.

"I . . . I don't know. Ya just are," she said. Vocalizing her finer emotions wasn't something she did effortlessly. She could count the times she'd been asked how she felt about something, on one hand with three fingers missing.

"Well, ya don't act like you're afraid of me," he said more to himself than to her. He coughed twice in his fist, then asked, "So, is it that you don't like men in general or just me in particular?"

But she did like him . . . to a certain extent. . . .

Certainly as much as she could allow herself to like anyone. Still . . .

"No. I think maybe I do like ya," she said cautiously. "You been good to me, and I thank ya." She hesitated. "I just don't know why."

"Why?" He made it sound like a foreign word.

"Yeah. Why are ya bein' nice to me? I ain't kin. Ya don't even know me. I keep waitin'—" she stopped abruptly and looked away.

"Waitin' for what?"

She glanced at him and lowered her eyes again. She'd never been given anything without something being expected in return. Most often, she'd been given food, shelter, and clothing in exchange for her labor. But there had been times when more was demanded of her.

"Waitin' for what, Ellis?" he asked a second time, his voice gentle and reassuring, his suspicions and fears climbing. "Do ya think I'm bein' nice to you 'cuz I wanna get ya in bed with me? Is that what ya think?"

She couldn't look at him, let alone admit the truth. What else did she have, that someone like Bryce LaSalle could possibly want?

"I usually think long and hard before I lie to someone, Ellis," he said, leaning closer so she wouldn't miss what he said. "And I just plain don't wanna lie to you." He paused briefly. "I think you're about the prettiest girl I've ever seen in my life, and I sure wouldn't complain if ya wanted to be with me. But the truth is, I don't want ya if you're thinkin' that you're payin' off a debt."

Her peek at him turned to an all-out stare when she realized he was in earnest. There was no humor, no twinkling in his deep-set eyes. No grin on his lips. What would his lips taste like? she wondered, shifting her weight against a sudden throbbing sensation between her legs, her heart pounding.

"Why, then?" she asked, hardly aware that she'd voiced the question. "Why are ya here? Why are ya helpin' me? Why are ya bein' so nice?"

He released a soft, incredulous laugh—as if he were as baffled by her as she was by him.

"I guess 'cuz I want to," he said. "Like in the bible where it says it's better to give than to receive. I feel better givin' than I do takin'."

"So I'm . . . charity." The word stuck in her throat.

"No!" he said, quickly denying what he didn't feel. "It ain't that at all. It's . . ."

"I don't need charity and I don't need your pity," she said, her spine as straight as a lightning rod.

"Pity?" He smothered another cough in his fist.

"I don't need nobody's help. I'm strong and able and I can tend for myself."

He leaned back to get a good look at her, a dazed expression on his face. When he could think of something to say, he said it.

"Fine. You're takin' it all wrong, but you have it your way, little prickly bush. I told Anne she was wastin' her time worryin' about you," he said, irate and not trying to hide it. Lord, she was like a burr under his skin, making *him* angry every time he rubbed *her* wrong. "I told her no self-respectin' masher would bother with someone as unfriendly as you, but no, I had to get up out of my sickbed," he coughed again for emphasis, "and drive all the way down here to check on you."

"Check on me? How come?"

"She didn't think Looty'd put you to work directly. She was expectin' ya to come home and unpack and settle in. She was hopin' you'd take a nap before ya came to work tonight."

"A nap?" She hadn't taken a nap during the day since she was three years old. Still, it was . . . nice of Anne to concern herself.

"Anne." He said the name with an amused tolerance, as if he thought her crazy but harmless. "She thought you looked tired this mornin'. And she doesn't think you're eatin' proper, thinks you're too thin." His lively green eyes caught her attention before he purposefully allowed his gaze to lower and lazily peruse the condition of her petite form. "Might have to stand up twice to get a good shadow, at that. And you do look tired. But if what Looty and Tug have been sayin' about ya is true, ya would."

"Lord a'mighty! You been talkin' to everybody about me?"

"No." He wagged his face in hers. "I got better things to do, Miss Prickly. I happen to be sick. I feel like hell, and all I wanna do is go to bed," he told her. "But I care about Anne, and *she* sent me out lookin' for ya. So I started at the beginnin' and called the diner. Ya think I enjoyed listenin' to Looty go on and on about how you're the hardest workin' girl she's ever seen? Like I was interested? Then I get the same stuff from Tug when I come here. And all I came to find out was what your plans were so I could tell Anne when you're comin' home."

Ellis was a bit stunned. Despite their delivery, she'd just received a bushel of kind words.

"They said that about me?" she asked in wonder.

He studied her with the curious expression she was growing used to seeing on his face. Her sudden pleasure baffled him.

"They did," he said softly, as if he'd never been angry or put out in his life.

She took a moment to savor the pride and satisfaction she was feeling, then remembered something else.

"I'm sorry I made Anne worry. We were goin' to list out the chores she wanted doin'. I shoulda used Looty's phone to call her." She hesitated, thinking of warmth, a bed, and safety. She sighed heavily. "I reckon I should move on and let Anne hire someone who can help her proper. I ain't sure I'll have the time now, 'tween the other two jobs."

"That's up to you and Anne," he said, placing his faith in Anne's art of persuasion to keep Ellis from moving out until she was better prepared. "The two of you can chew on it after supper."

"No, we can't."

His dark brows rose in question.

"See, that's the thing," she said, feeling guilty for accepting a job she wouldn't be able to carry out. "When Mr. Hogan's short on help for nights, I can stay on and work extra. I need the money more than I need a bed."

His eyes narrowed keenly. "You're plannin' to work eighteen hours a day?"

"Any time I can," she said, uncomfortable under his intense gaze. "I told ya I needed money. I need it in a hurry. And your sister-in-law oughta get someone she can count on."

"How long are ya plannin' to work like this? How much money do ya need?" He'd known men to work long days to pay off hospital bills or gambling debts or lawyers, but only when the debt was urgent. "Are you sure you're not in trouble?"

It wasn't any of his concern how much money she needed or what it was for or how she went about earning it, but she somehow felt compelled to tell him.

"I need one thousand five hundred thirty-six dollars and eighty-seven cents." She shrugged. "More if you take in a place to live and a bit to fall back on."

"You're savin' for a new car?"

"No." She frowned and looked thoughtful, her guard slipping away unnoticed. "Though I expect I'll be lookin' in that direction soon enough. The truck needs a fine hand to keep it runnin', and I ain't at all mechanical minded."

"Then what do ya need all that money for?"

She looked at him and realized that she'd opened her door too wide. Yet sharing what little she had had felt good.

"It's personal," she said, not unkindly. "A debt. So I can get back what's mine."

He considered this, and then shook his head. "You can't work yourself to death payin' off a debt. It ain't like it'll get up and walk away."

"I ain't workin' myself to death."

"The hell you ain't. Look at yourself. You're pale, too thin, and ya can hardly stand up straight you're so tired."

"I'm okay."

"Like hell," he said, turning to look down the bar at Tug Hogan. "Hey, Tug," he bellowed, and when the man turned to look at him, he said, "You gonna need Ellis all night or can she leave early?"

"No," she said, frantic as Tug walked to their end of the bar. "No. Don't say nothin'. This ain't your concern."

"There a problem here?" Tug asked, standing on the other side of the bar from them.

"No," she stated emphatically.

"Yes," Bryce said just as vehemently. "She's workin' herself sick. She needs to sleep."

Tug's hooded gaze passed to Ellis. She squirmed beneath his scrutiny, finally bursting forth with, "I can do the work."

"I know," he said. "But I won't be needin' ya after midnight."

"But I"—he turned his back on her and walked away—"need the money," she said, her words dwindling to a bare whisper as she realized the futility of arguing. She turned to Bryce with murder in her eyes. "Look what ya done!"

"Tug's a good ol' boy. He wouldn't have let ya go if it wasn't as plain as the nose on his face that you're as wrung out as yesterday's dish towel." He thought he saw tears welling in her eyes before she looked heavenward and closed them in an effort to control herself. Instantly contrite, he tried to soothe her. "He ain't holdin' nothing against ya. Tug likes ya."

"What about the money?" she asked, refusing to be soothed.

"How much money can ya make in a place like this in two hours? And is it worth makin' yourself sick for it?" he asked. "Where's your head, for chrissake?"

"It's mindin' its own business," she said, taking note

of a customer who was trying to get her attention. "And that's more than I can say for yours. You just leave me alone, ya hear?"

"Fine," he said as she turned to go. "Don't dawdle on your way home. Anne goes to bed early these days, so I'll have to wait up to show ya your room."

She turned to face him. "Don't put yourself out. I ain't plannin' on takin' the job, so I won't be stayin' the night. I'll call Anne in the mornin' and tell her so myself."

"Fine," he said. "You just keep on doin' what you gotta do, and I'll do the same."

He stalked out of the bar, his fingers itching to shake some sense into her head. She was a devil in disguise. She looked like an angel, but he was sure God never intended any of his celestial sidekicks to be as stubborn, willful, wrongheaded, or irritating as Ellis. Ellis . . . ? What the hell was her last name? he wondered, stopping dead in his tracks in the parking lot to look back at the Steel Wheel with a sudden flash of inspiration.

Ellis wanted to kick herself, but then she didn't. She was glad to see him go, but then she wasn't. She was seething with anger, but she'd never felt more special or worried over. She was sick to her stomach from the ups and down of her emotions. Bryce had a way of making her want to spit fire, swoon with excitement, scream with indignation, weep with happiness, and tear her hair out in confusion all at once.

And she didn't feel any better six hours later when she let herself out of the Steel Wheel, dreading another night of sleeping in the truck. She could have spent the night in a bed, she reminded herself. She shook her head and quickly reinforced her earlier conclusions that she wouldn't have been much help to Anne and, more importantly, the greater the distance she put between Bryce and herself, the better off she'd be.

She climbed into the truck and rubbed her hands together, warming them before touching the ice-cold steering wheel. She'd finished the ritual of the first engine turnover before it registered in her mind that something was wrong.

Her blanket was gone. And so was the old carpetbag that held the only material possessions she owned. A weak cry of terror escaped her throat as she scrambled around to reach down the back of the seat for her bankroll. It was gone.

Too stunned to cry, she slumped back behind the steering wheel trying to catch her breath and calm her heart. Why would anyone rob someone so poor, they couldn't buy hay for a nightmare? The money she could understand, but the holey blanket? her mother's old books? the pictures? the rest of . . .

The realization hit her so hard, it made her head ache. A good thief would have taken the money and run without hampering his escape with a bunch of old rags and books that were worthless. Bryce would have taken everything just to spite her.

Five

Despite the frigid weather, the roads were clear of ice and snow. The old pickup truck peeled around curves, zoomed uphill and took flight in the depression dips as it climbed higher into the mountains. She missed the unmarked entrance to the LaSalle property, but even after backtracking she stood on the front porch of the LaSalle home in record time.

Ellis was angry enough to chew nails and spit rivets. Knocking on the door seemed timid and mousy considering her mood. She wanted to boot the door open, but Bryce opened it before she had the chance.

"Well, that didn't take ya long to figure out," he said, grinning as if he had good sense. "I like a clever woman."

"Gimme my stuff," she said through clenched teeth. He was a big, handsome thief, and her body automatically responded to him, rioting with delight and womanly urges. But, devil take him, she was fire-spewin', arm-wavin', butt-chewin' mad. She wanted to punch him. "I oughta shoot ya."

"What? With your make-believe gun?" he asked, not bothering to hide his enjoyment. "Why don't ya stab me and save your bullets?"

She growled at him. "I trusted ya. I thought ya a

friend, and this is how ya treat me. You'd steal flies from a blind spider."

"The hell I would. And you ain't the one to be speakin' on the way friends treat each other." He coughed, harsh and long. "Come on in and scream at me. It's cold out here."

"Just gimme my stuff."

"No. Come inside."

Well, it *was* cold, and she didn't think she'd win a fistfight with him. She stepped past him and stood as straight and tall as an oak tree, just inside the door. She spied her possessions stacked neatly on the floor at the bottom of the stairwell. Her money bag was on top and in full view. She snatched it and proceeded to count the contents.

Bryce leaned against the wall to watch her, and when she was satisfied that not a penny was missing, she stuffed the bag in her coat pocket and glowered at him. He was ghost pale and looked weak as he supported himself against the wall. He was not too weak to speak, however.

"Nice show of trust there," he said. "Do ya really think I'd steal from ya?"

"Ya did." She showed him the evidence.

He shook his head. "I was just leading the horse . . . the *mule* to water. I didn't get into nothin'." He coughed and came close to falling over before he could catch his breath. Ellis took an unthinking step forward to help him, but he held up a hand to stop her, saying, "I wanted ya to stay here. I made a mess of everything at the Wheel and I'm sorry. I didn't set out to meddle in your business. I . . ." Once more he broke into a spasm of coughing before he could finish. "I was trying to help. I'm sorry."

"What?"

He presented her with a forlorn expression, as if willing but incapable of repeating his words. He paraphrased, "I said I was sorry."

No child, no woman, and certainly no man had ever

uttered those words to her before. Lord knew, they were common enough to her lips, but she never in her life dreamed she'd hear them coming her way twice in one day.

"You're sick," she said, her chest aching with a peculiar but not unpleasant fullness.

He scowled, misunderstanding her. "I said I was sorry and that's all the apologizin' I aim to do. Take your things and go, if it's what ya want. I'm past caring where ya sleep."

"You're dead and too stupid to fall over, is what ya are," she said, just as sternly, taking matters into her own hands. She took him by the arm, led him over to the couch, and fairly pushed him into it, though it didn't take much effort.

He moaned. Horizontal agreed with him, returning a small fraction of his color. It was also a natural position in which to close one's eyes.

"Stood out in the cold too long last night," he muttered to no one in particular.

"You shoulda skedaddled when I told ya to. Bet now ya wished ya had," she said, placing a tentative touch to his brow. He peeked through thick, dark lashes at her and shook his head slowly. The heat he was generating amazed her. She allowed her hand to settle on his forehead.

"Cold hands, warm heart," he mumbled, a small smile on his lips.

"You're dreamin'," she said softly.

"Hearin' ya talk sweet and gentle, maybe I am." He opened one eye to watch her response and chuckled when she frowned. "It was a nice dream."

"You're whipped down with a punishin' fever. You should be in bed. Have ya taken any medicine?"

"In a minute," he said. "Just let me lay here a second more . . . then I'll leave."

"Leave? Where ya goin'?"

"The other house. I moved my things back this

mornin'. Wanted ya to feel easy here." He sighed. "I'll go in a minute."

"Ya can't drive like this."

"Okay. I'll walk."

"How far? Where is this other house? I didn't see another for miles this mornin'."

"Woods. Couple hundred yards behind this one. Pretty place. All mine."

Trying to help him back to his house in his present condition would be as futile as pushing a wheelbarrow with rope handles, she speculated. He was twice her size and as weak and helpless as a baby.

"Where'd ya sleep last night?"

"My room. Upstairs."

"Come on," she said, standing to pull on his arm, taking note of his shivering. "I'll help ya up the stairs. Ya got a right smart shake there."

"You ain't gonna sleep in that damn truck, are ya?" he asked, slowly getting to his feet with her aid.

"Maybe not tonight. Watch your step." She pulled his arm across her shoulders and pressed her weight upward to hold him steady. "Did ya take somethin' for the fever?"

"Aspirin. I don't think it's workin'."

"Never does." She gasped with exertion, placing his free hand on the banister. "Where'n tarnation is your kin? Don't they know you're ailin'?"

"Came on after they went to bed," he said, leaning heavily on the handrail to catch his breath. He laughed softly, then coughed and chuckled, saying, "Told 'em I took your stuff. Told 'em you'd be mad as hellfire when ya got here, and not to bother gettin' up 'less they heard me screamin' in pain."

"Like I could hurt ya." Was there nothing he wouldn't say? "Come on. The sooner ya get there, the sooner ya can lay down again."

"It's mighty nice of ya to help me like this, Ellis." He paused. "But I suppose you're only doin' it to get me into bed."

Hadn't she just told him where he needed to be? He was loosing his mind to the fever, she decided.

"That's right," she said. "Ya need—" She stopped when a snort of humor escaped him. She had to slip out from under his arm or be pulled down with him as he started to crumple on the steps with laughter. She stood for a second or two, deeply concerned by the madness in his mind until she recalled their earlier conversation at the Steel Wheel.

Relieved that he wasn't as far gone with the fever as she had imagined, she hoped that between the coughing and hooting he'd choke to death for throwing her suspicions of his good deeds back in her face.

"Ah, Ellis, you sweet little thing," he said, gasping and chuckling intermittently. "Ya gotta get a sense of humor."

"Fool."

"Sorry," he said, though she could tell he was far from it. "I'm dizzy and feverish. I can't help it." She humphed and pulled on his arm to get him started again. He went right on talking.

"But I'm not completely senseless yet. I know why you're helpin' me like this." He bent his head below his armpit to see her face. "Ya pity me. I'm your act of charity for the day. Ain't that right? 'Cuz I know you wouldn't help somebody just because ya believe in one person bein' kind to another for no reason other than it's how things oughta be—Oops." He fell heavily against her and the wall. "Since we're all pretty much in the same boat."

"Why don't ya rest your mouth," she said, acutely conscious of the length and breadth of his overheated body pressed against hers. She struggled to keep them both from falling to the bottom of the stairs. "Mind what you're doin' here."

"I am. And I like it," he said, his voice low and seductive.

She strained under his weight to look at him. He was grinning like a hog in slop. In the time it took her to blink, a familiar light in his fever-glazed eyes stirred panic within her and brought the taste of salt and bile to the back of her throat. She was ready to scream, but when she blinked again the spark was gone.

"Which room is yours?" she asked breathlessly, forcing her voice to sound calm.

With a hand to the wall on either side of her, Bryce pushed himself away from her.

"Ellis?"

"What?" she answered absently, her hands on his waist in a vain attempt to turn him to the top of the stairs.

"Look at me." When she did, he squeezed his eyes closed as if trying to refocus them. When he reopened them, they were bright and glassy and filled with concern. "Why are ya tremblin' like that?"

"You're heavy. I thought I was gonna drop ya." Had she imagined that look in his eyes? Or had her memory been playing tricks on her? No. Blurry-eyed men with a raging fever were just as unpredictable as blurry-eyed men drunk on corn liquor, she reminded herself. She tried to smile at him. "Let's give it another shot here, huh?"

"Did I scare ya?"

"'Course not," she lied. "We'll get on fine now if ya could just get turned 'round a bit."

"Ellis."

"What?"

"Don't lie to me. Look at ya. You're shaking like a leaf in the wind."

"That's 'cuz you're makin' me mad again," she said, a might sharp. "Think I got nothin' better to do than to stand on these here steps jawin' with ya?"

Abruptly, he pushed away from the wall and sagged into a heap at her feet. With his elbows on his knees, he supported his head on his fists, shaking it back and forth slowly.

"I scared ya," he said sadly. "If I ever do somethin' that makes ya happy, will ya tell me?"

Ellis stood in half wonderment, half horror. Bryce LaSalle was the oddest man she'd ever come across, and there was no making heads or tails of him. Why would he want to do something to make her happy? Why would he care? More important at the moment, however, was what to do with him?

She was visually measuring the distance to the top of the stairs and contemplating a scream for help when he started talking again.

"You're the oddest female I've ever come across, and for the life of me, I can't make heads or tails of ya."

Ellis couldn't stop it. She laughed out loud.

"*That's* funny?" he asked, looking up at her, plainly thinking that her wit was badly warped.

Amused and smiling, she slid down the wall to sit beside him. "I was just thinkin' the same thing about you."

"You were?" He returned her smile. "That is funny, 'cuz I ain't a bit odd."

She laughed again.

"When you laugh it's like listenin' to music. Soft and full of life and energy," he said, growing serious. "And I swear I never saw anything prettier than the way you look when ya smile like that."

Oh! He set her cheeks on fire and her heart to racing. Hummingbirds took wing in her abdomen, and, curiously, she wanted to cry. Lordy, this man said the most uncommon things at the most peculiar moments. Taking no chances, she put her hand to his brow and found it burning hot.

"I'll laugh for ya again tomorrow. But if we don't tend to this fever, you're gonna get brain fried," she said, regretfully dismissing his sweet talk as delirium. A man was likely to say most anything when he was pegged out with a sickness.

"Auk!" he bellowed as if pained by a frustration he could no longer tolerate. "There ya go again! Disregardin' what I say like I don't know beans from bird eggs or straight up when I see it."

"Well, when ya talk like that I wonder if ya do," she said, standing to pull on his arm once again, refusing to believe he was anywhere near sane. "You are the *beatin'est* man."

"At least I ain't prickly."

"Ha! Every time I open my mouth ya fly off in every which direction."

"I don't. You ask anyone who knows me. I'm known for bein' slow goin' and easy tempered."

"This little girl hurtin' you, Bryce?" came Buck's voice from the top of the stairs. "I heard ya yellin' and came runnin'."

Ellis and Bryce turned to look at him. His flannel robe was tied askew and his hair was rumpled. He was straight-faced, but it didn't look as if he could hold in his mirth much longer.

They both spoke at once.

"Lord in heaven, am I glad to see ya. I need help."

"Tell her how slow goin' and easy tempered I am."

"He's slow goin' and easy tempered," Buck said in a dry matter-of-fact tone of voice as he stepped down to help Ellis drag his brother up the few remaining stairs to the top.

"She thinks she's the only one who can look at a fistful of fingers and count five," Bryce complained, falling back on the landing like a dead man and closing his eyes with a weary groan.

"Oh, that's not very nice," Anne said, joining the party. "Bryce can count ten fingers if he uses two hands."

"See, Miss Prickly," Bryce said without looking at her. "Tell her I know pretty when I see it too."

"He does," they said, nodding at each other in agreement.

"The poison from his sickness is givin' him a fever. I think his brain's goin' soft," Ellis said, too relieved to see Anne and Buck to pay heed to the strange way they talked. "I was tryin' to get him into a bed."

"But not for what you're thinkin' and not because she

likes me," Bryce spoke up from the floor without opening his eyes. "She's feelin' pity for me."

Ellis sighed and rolled her eyes.

"Ya do look a bit peaked, brother," Buck said, leaning over him for a closer look. He slid his hands under his brother's arms and started dragging him toward a door on the left.

"I caught a chill standing out in the cold last night," Bryce explained offhandedly, hardly aware of what was happening to him. "My bones ache. I wanna die. Maybe I shoulda let her shoot me."

Anne had gone to a closet down the hall and returned with clean sheets.

"Let who shoot you?" she asked, following the men into Bryce's room and silently asking Ellis to help her make up the bed.

"Ellis."

Ellis blushed hot all over when Anne and Buck looked at her.

She shrugged. "I mighta," she said truthfully. "But I ain't got a gun."

"She ain't got a knife either," Bryce said, sounding drowsy as Buck lowered him carefully to the floor beside the bed, straddling each leg to remove his boots. "But she can skin a pig with that tongue of hers."

Anne started to laugh. From the other side of the bed she smiled at Ellis and finished tucking in the sheets. "If he weren't so sick, I could really love this. I don't think he's talked this much in all the time I've known him."

"That caps the stack," Ellis said, amazed. "Chews my ears till they're close to bleedin' every chance he gets. And he's so dang ornery, I . . ."

"Bryce?" Anne frowned. "Why, there isn't an ornery bone in his body, Ellis. He's the sweetest, gentlest man I've ever met." When Buck muttered something under the strain of removing his brother's boots, she added, "After you, sweetheart."

Buck shot his wife a dazzling grin and a look so

bursting with love that it pulled at something shallow and selfish inside Ellis. She wished that just once in her life someone would smile at her in the same way.

Bryce groaned in misery, and the women stepped up the pace of their efforts. When the bed was made, Buck and Ellis each took an arm, urging Bryce up off the floor and onto the clean sheets. She couldn't settle her gaze on any one object in the room when Buck reached for the buttons on his brother's blue denims. He stepped to the end of the bed and began to pull off Bryce's socks and pants.

Ellis was hypnotized by the slow movement of the waistband hugging Bryce's hips. It inched away to reveal lean flesh still golden brown from the summer sun, and a thin line of coarse dark hair that tapered lower and lower. . . .

"I'll get the aspirin and some cold cloths," she heard Anne say, shattering the direction of her thoughts. She released a breath that she hadn't realized she'd been holding and quickly followed Anne from the room.

"He . . . he took aspirin before," she stammered, not wanting to overstep her boundaries in a place where she didn't belong, but wanting to be helpful just the same. "It didn't much help. I . . . could I tend him? I ain't got the power, but I've had trainin' tendin' the sick. I . . . I think I can help him."

"Of course you can. Shall I get some ice? I think there's some—"

"Where's your root cellar?"

"The root cellar?"

Ellis nodded. "Ya got a barn or an outshack? A tool shed maybe?"

It was a skeptical Anne LaSalle who gave Ellis the information she was asking for and directed her to her specific needs. She watched in bewilderment as Ellis cut onions and dropped them into a pot of boiling water, and she scurried off to find flannel when she was asked to, though she wasn't sure why. With a grimace she watched Ellis sauté one of the onions in butter until it was clear and soft and then added sugar to it, stirring until the mixture was a thick syrup.

With the four cloth diapers that Anne had taken from the supply she'd gathered for her baby, the pot of boiled onions, and a small jar of the onion syrup, Ellis returned to the sickroom on the second floor.

"This is likely to take a spell," she said when Anne and Buck seemed reluctant to leave Bryce's side. "But I don't need more than one other body to do it."

"You know," Anne said in a high, rather nervous voice, "I was wondering about taking him to the hospital."

Anne's skepticism hurt. In Stony Hollow she'd become inured to distrust. Yet coming from Anne it was like something new. She looked at Bryce. He was shivering, no longer pale, but flushed with the heat of his fever. The sight of his bare, hair-covered chest did fascinating things to her innards.

It did occur to her that if he went to the hospital, she could get four full hours of sleep before morning. She was spent and drained. But she also knew she'd never sleep again if she didn't follow her conscience.

"I told ya that I ain't got the healin' power like some, but I've tended worse off than him," she said. "It's high time to break his fever, and I can do it if ya say to, but . . . it's for y'all to choose."

Buck gave his wife a one-armed hug and kissed her lightly on the temple, saying, "Go back to bed, Annie. Ya need your sleep. I'll help Ellis." Anne hesitated. "Go on now. Ellis can handle this."

Ellis can handle this. Let Ellis do this. She'd heard the sentiment of his words a thousand times. There had always been a job for Ellis. Cooking, cleaning, mending, plowing, chopping, hauling, pushing, pulling . . . But when Buck said the words "Ellis can handle this," it didn't sound the same. It didn't sound like, give this job to Ellis, it's all she's good for. Or, this is your job, Ellis, because I don't want to do it.

When Buck said those words, it was more like a vote

of confidence. It was as if he were saying, this is something Ellis can do that we can't—it's important to let her do it.

"I can," she said, nodding a heartfelt thank you to Buck that he didn't see and probably wouldn't have understood. She smiled reassuringly at Anne. Being from the north would explain Anne's uncertainty, she decided tolerantly. She wouldn't understand mountain ways the way Buck did.

"Okay. Call if you need me," Anne said, smiling at Ellis.

If Anne wasn't sure of Ellis's methods, she certainly had no reservations about her husband's. Such trust was noteworthy, Ellis thought, eyeing Buck as they stood facing each other over Bryce's bed.

"Onion poultice, right?" he asked. She nodded, and he chuckled. "Then we'd best get him while he's too weak to fight it."

Ellis found Buck to be an extremely able assistant. He got another sheet and folded it narrow, rolling his drowsy brother back and forth across it, leaving both ends free. With expert hands, she deftly placed the hot onion layers in one half of one of the diapers, folded the remaining cloth around them, and slipped it under Bryce's back before Buck rolled him over to lay on it. She quickly made another dressing for his chest and drew the ends of the sheeting tightly over it to hold in the heat.

They covered him with two more blankets, and while Buck held the invalid's head, she poured a spoonful of the onion cough syrup down his throat.

"Awk! What are ya doin' to me?" Bryce muttered feebly. His eyes rolled open, and he looked from Ellis to Buck before they closed again. "That smell. It's hurtin' my eyes."

"Shut your yap and stop complainin'," Buck told him, not unsympathetically. "The onions stink, but your nurse is pretty. Settle back and enjoy it."

A smile curved one side of Bryce's mouth, then drooped.

"She thinks she owes me for something," he muttered. "Otherwise she'd let me die."

"A lot you know," she said, wondering if giving up her sleep had been such a wise decision after all. Lordy, how could anyone so sick be so contrary . . . and so appealing? "If ya think ya can sleep between the changes, I'll bicker with him till he falls back to sleep," she said, addressing herself to Buck.

He nodded, smiling, and turned to leave without comment.

The door closed, and Ellis sighed, knowing there was nothing left to do but wait for the fever to break. Carefully, so as not to disturb him, she sat down on the bed beside Bryce with nothing but time to muse over the night's events.

It would be easy and very wonderful for her to take Bryce at face value, to believe every word he said, and to believe that he had no ulterior motive for his kindness toward her. She wanted to think that he liked her, not as an object of his lust or as someone to be pitied or as someone of potential use to him, simply as Ellis—a person with feelings and thoughts of her own.

No one knew the real Ellis except Ellis. She wasn't sure when she had become the great pretender she was, but in Stony Hollow what she felt, thought, and did behind people's backs had been very different from the way she'd acted in their presence.

She was seven before she knew the truth of her birth and finally figured out why she never seemed to fit in anywhere. The woman she called mama was the real mother of three sons slightly older than Ellis. She was a widow woman who lived with her older brother, and her name was Effie Watson.

Effie was the kindest woman she had ever known. The only time Effie spoke to her of her birth was when Ellis had asked, and she never treated Ellis any differ-

ently than she did her own children, though there had
been some contention with her brother.

Her birth-mother had been a young, middle-class
woman who'd come into the mountains of eastern
Kentucky to teach the poverty-stricken children. Ac-
cording to Effie, Stephanie Ellis hadn't been prepared
for what she'd found. She'd tried, Effie had insisted, to
overcome her middle-class standards and relate to the
people she'd come to help. But folks didn't cotton to
what they considered her condescending attitude and
snooty ways, and by the time she'd met Effie, only a few
would have anything to do with her.

Effie seemed to understand her, and they got along
famously. Stephanie started to teach her and her oldest
boy to read, and Effie tried to explain mountain ways
and spread goodwill toward her in return. And then
Stephanie had turned up pregnant.

She'd refused to name the father, and speculation
had run rampant until the young Vista worker had
been completely isolated from the community—the
men not wanting to be accused by association, the
women protective and jealous of their husbands and
sons, the younger women afraid of catching her disgrace. Only Effie, a widow, whose sons were too young
to be involved, had befriended Stephanie.

She'd sworn that she'd done all she could for Stephanie when "female problems" had interfered with the
delivery of the baby. Stephanie died two days later,
leaving a sickly, undersized girl behind. With no one
else to care whether the baby lived or died, and a secret
wish for a baby girl of her own, Effie had taken the child
in against her brother's wishes and had named her
Ellis.

Because Effie's brother cared for her, he'd tolerated
Ellis's presence in his home. It wasn't until Tommy Lee
Tucker had thrashed her soundly after school one day
and recalled for the entire schoolyard the circumstances of her birth that Ellis had discovered why her

"uncle" had never been as loving with her as he had been with his nephews.

Bryce moaned and threw off his covers. He went for the bandage on his chest, and she gently but firmly held his hands away. He didn't put up much of a fight.

"Shh. Ya rest now," she said softly. "You'll need your strength later, for fightin' the poison in your body."

"Ellis," he mumbled, weakly coughing the grog from his throat.

"Go back to sleep, Bryce." She put his hands to his sides and brought the blankets back up to his neck. His left arm battled its way out again, and when she moved to replace it, she felt his grip, astoundingly strong around her wrist.

"Ellis."

"It's Ellis," she said, as if he'd asked. "But don't start fightin' with me again. You ain't at your best, so I can stomp a mudhole in your chest, if ya give me any trouble."

"Tough as a cob, ain't ya?" he whispered, his eyes closed.

"Sometimes ya gotta be."

"Why?"

"So ya don't get crushed," she said simply. His hand relaxed at her wrist and slipped into hers.

Ellis tucked the covers up close to his shoulders, leaving his left arm exposed, his hand in hers. Impulsively, she stroked his upper arm. She caressed him again. And once again, because touching him fascinated her. His skin was hot and smooth over ice-hard muscle. Even in sleep, his body lax and unguarded, he was solid and brawny, grand and impressive. Ellis took liberties, letting her eyes and fingers stray, liking what she saw and felt.

What would it feel like to be held in arms that were as strong and powerful as Bryce's? she wondered. Would he touch her gently and whisper sweet words to her? Would he kiss her tenderly? Would his eyes shine with love and happiness? Would he cherish her, care for her, protect her?

She jumped from the bed, dropping his hand like a hot potato, when he began to move restlessly, saying, "Hot. Too hot."

"I . . . I know," she said, feeling guilty for her thoughts. Even if Bryce had the slightest inclination to feel or do any one of the things she'd been dreaming about, she couldn't for a second forget that she had a prior commitment to someone who meant the earth, the moon, and the stars to her. And there was Liddy Evans to consider. . . .

She dampened a cloth in a bowl of cool water and pressed it to his cheeks and forehead. For long minutes she cooled his furrowed brow, smoothing his thick, dark hair from his temple, thinking him to be asleep. When he reached up and took her hand in his, she watched his face to see if he would look at her. He didn't.

"Ellis?"

"Yes?"

"Thanks."

There was something thick and heavy in her throat. She tried to swallow around it and her chin quivered. Lordy! What nonsense, she chided herself, taking the cloth into her other hand to fold it across his forehead.

The hand she held easily in hers caught her attention. Instead of putting it under the covers to ward off any further flimflam, she covered the long, work-worn fingers with her own and turned her thoughts in another direction.

Effie Watson's fingers had been fat and stubby, but calloused like Bryce's. They had been special hands. Gentle when they'd brushed the tangles from Ellis's too-long and too-thick blond hair. Kind when they'd patted a kiss into Ellis's cheek before bed every night.

Until Ellis was eleven she'd depended on Effie and her hands for protection. And Effie had tried. She'd done her best to make up for all the ills and prejudices of the world, to make Ellis feel loved and wanted, but nothing was ever quite the same once the truth had been told.

She missed Effie. She could still feel the pain she'd known in the days following the fateful morning of Effie's accident. Every soul in Stony Hollow descended on the Talbot-Watson home in grief and sorrow after hearing that a tree had fallen on the dear, kind-hearted woman. But nary a one had had a kind word for the young girl whose heart and future had died with her.

Effie's beloved family muddled along for as long as they could, but a bachelor with four children soon became a hopeless case. Finding it impossible to work and feed and tend the children as well, Effie's brother had been forced to turn to his family for help. His second sister had been willing to take the boys into her home, but Ellis wasn't kin and she was baseborn to boot.

"I promise to be good," Ellis had sobbed, clinging to her oldest brother, hoping he'd never let go of her. "I'll work hard and I won't eat nothin', I promise."

"Let go of her, boy," Uncle Cal had said quietly. "She can't go."

"She ain't no trouble," Bobby'd said, his pubescent voice cracking at the edges with emotion.

"We'll take care of her. We'll share our food," the other boys had chimed in, the younger one wiping his teary eyes and nose on the sleeve of his shirt.

"She ain't one of us," Cal said. "She ain't kin. Faylyn don't know her like we do." He'd pried Ellis from her brother's arms. "There's no need to carry on now. I promised your ma that I'd make sure she was cared for, and I will."

Ellis had been sure that her heart was torn and bleeding inside her. Uncle Cal had promised to fetch the boys back when he could, but they were all mountain kids and knew the way of things. Nothing would be the same again.

Six

Ellis heard Buck in the hallway before he touched the door handle. She was standing across the room near the window when he stuck his head into the room.

"It's been an hour. Is it time to change those onion plasters?"

She nodded him into the room. "I changed the top one a half hour ago. I been waitin' on ya." She picked up the kettle of boiled onions.

"Shoulda called," Buck said, walking over to the bed to check on his brother.

"There was no need before now," she said, admiring Buck's obvious concern for Bryce. "Changing one dressin' at a time is best, so as to draw the fever out gradual, but I needed to heat these up, and I was wary of leavin' him alone for long."

"He behavin'?"

"Never had a better patient," she said, letting go with one of her rare smiles. "Too bad he ain't so mannerly when he's feelin' fit."

"He's not?"

Ellis had meant to be humorous, for contrary to what Bryce thought of her, she did like a good joke. But she'd only managed to confuse Buck. It was as if they were speaking about two different people.

"No, he ain't. Not to me, least ways," she said. "He's nosy and nasty and flies into a snit over the tiniest things." She paused thoughtfully. "'Course, he laughs at the wrong times and he's understandin' when he oughta be spittin' mad, and . . . I don't mean to be badmouthin' your kin and all, but tryin' to figure out what he'll do next is like tryin' to lick honey off a blackberry vine."

She was reassured by a slow, knowing grin on Buck's face.

"Well, I expect if anyone can handle him, you can," he said, looking down at Bryce. "And he ain't half bad once ya get to know him."

She nodded but didn't respond. She didn't want to handle Bryce, and she didn't have time to get to know him. She had a fortune to earn, and he was getting in her way . . . muddling her thoughts, confusing her body, tormenting her emotions.

They put a fresh onion poultice to Bryce's back, removing the first with the onions now looking fried rather than boiled. Buck asked if there was anything else he could do and, receiving her negative response, turned to go back to bed.

"Are ya sure ya wouldn't like to get some sleep?" he asked at the door. "I'd call ya if anything changed."

"Thanks, but it'll be over soon. I'll stay."

She had no hope of seeing the bed she'd been promised any time soon. Bryce was restless at times, but not thrashing. He'd mumble and complain of aching or being too hot or of a terrible cold and drift back to sleep.

She sat in a chair next to the window for the next hour, staring off into space. Well . . . she might have dozed off for a second or two, but she was wide awake when she heard Buck's footsteps in the hall again. They changed the compresses as before, and during the third hour, beads of perspiration popped up on Bryce's face like dew drops. He soaked the bed linen and slept the next hour away in a deep, sound sleep with easy, regular respirations. The fever was beaten.

Shortly after dawn he awoke, making several attempts to get out of bed and cursing Ellis soundly when she impeded him.

"How can ya look as sweet as ya do and be so mean?" he complained, frowning furiously.

"Hush. You'll wake the others. You're talkin' loud enough to wake the dead."

"I feel like the dead," he said, falling back into the damp sheets with a groan. "Talk to me, Ellis. Only say somethin' nice for a change, so I can think of somethin' else besides the way I feel."

"You want a bedtime tale?" she asked, remembering someone else who liked them.

"Yeah. About Ellis. Tell me what ya dream of."

"I don't have dreams, just plans," she said, dismissing her dreams, loath to expose her weaknesses to anyone.

He studied her quietly. Several long seconds went by before he responded. "Then tell me about your plans."

"My plans."

"The money. What are ya goin' to do after you pay off your debt? Buy a big fancy house and one of those limousines? Or are ya goin' to move to California and dress up in jewels and animal furs?"

Her chuckle was quiet, but her grin was bold and bright.

"You're pretty enough to be a movie star," he said.

"And you're full of corn."

"Tell me what you're goin' to do with all that money. I swear I won't tell nobody."

Exhausted, her guard worn paper thin, she sat down on the bed beside him and dabbed at his brow with a cool damp cloth.

"Close your eyes," she said, wanting him to rest. "The money I'm savin' now is important 'cuz . . . well, 'cuz it is. I gotta go back to Stony Hollow to get what's mine. After that, I'll set about makin' a new life for myself," she said with fervor. "Since ya don't know me, I reckon you'd think I was hankerin' for a big house and fast cars and all that, but I ain't. I read in a magazine once about California. . . . There's things I'd like to see there, but I don't think I'd care much to live there. New York neither. Fact is, I think the best thing about livin' in the mountains is that there ain't too many people who do."

She folded the cloth neatly and placed it on his forehead before she turned away and continued to speak.

"See, most people don't cotton to me." ✓

"Why not?"

The truth had a way of coming back on a person, and no amount of lying or pretending could ever change it. She knew that if she didn't speak the truth now, she'd be taken for a liar later.

"I was a come-by-chance child. I been wearin' my mama's sin all my life."

Silence followed her confession. Rallying her pride, she turned to face him. His eyes were open and he was watching her again, not with the jaundice she was expecting but with insight, as if he knew every detail of her life without being told.

"Tell me about your plans," he said softly, simply, closing his eyes once more.

Was that it? she wondered, filled with pride and fightin' words that she wasn't going to need. Didn't he care who he invited into his home? Or who he let tend him?

"I . . . I been thinkin' on a small house here in the mountains somewhere. Someplace quiet and away from other people. Someplace new where no one knows me. But someplace where I can earn a livin', so I won't have to be on welfare. And someplace close to a school," she added as an imperative afterthought. "Gotta have a school."

She went silent, thoughtful on the power of an education, wishing she had one.

"School?" Bryce urged her, sounding half-asleep.

"I wanna go to school. I want a high school diploma," she said. "I ain't sure what I'd do at college, but maybe

I'd know if I finished high school. I mean, well, I wanna finish high school, and then if there's something special I wanna know about, I might wanna go to college too." She paused. "Anne went to school, didn't she?"

"Mmm," he mumbled.

"She's real smart, ain't she?"

"Like a tree full of owls."

"I like the way she talks. She talks educated."

"Talks a lot."

"So do you."

He opened one eye to peek at her. "Anne says the house is so quiet with just her and me in it, she has to cut on the radio or go nuts listenin' to dust fallin' on the furniture."

"Do tell. Well, she can take my end of your stick any day. You're always yapping at me."

"You need to be yapped at. She don't."

"Ya wanna hear the rest of my plans or not?"

"Yes," he said, closing his eye. "School, little house, no people."

She was debating how much more of her plan she was going to tell him when Buck entered the room.

"How's he doin'?" he asked. "Heard him hollerin' in here a while back, but I figured if you needed me, you'd start hollerin' too."

"Fever's broke and he's back to bein' peevish," she said, more in jest than serious. She'd actually enjoyed their last few minutes of conversation. It was nice to tell someone about her plans for the future, and to have that someone listen as if it mattered. "I reckon it's time for me to leave."

"No!" Bryce shouted, sitting straight up in bed.

"Where ya goin'?" Buck asked, much calmer than his brother. "You haven't slept all night."

"Don't I know it?" she said, standing to stretch her muscles. "But I got a job. It wouldn't do to miss my second day on a new job."

"Looty's? I could call her and explain. She'd give ya the time off . . . seein' as Bryce is the only young fellah in town who still flirts with her."

She turned an incredulous expression on Bryce. "You flirt with Looty too?"

"She makes great biscuits," he said, lying back down on the bed. "Will ya come back here when you're done?"

"I think you should sleep, Ellis," Buck said. "Ya look worn out."

"Save your breath, Buck," Bryce said in a resigned tone. "Ya can't reason with her. She's got plans. The best we can do is just hang around to pick up the pieces when she falls apart."

"You can fetch me some turpentine, if ya have any," she told Buck, ignoring Bryce's words. "Make him stay in bed and sleep today. And give him lots of water to drink. He don't need the plasters no more, but he should have the cough medicine every few hours or he'll cough his fool head off."

"You ever taste that stuff you been pourin' down my throat?"

"You ever been quiet for more'n five minutes?"

Both men were quiet by nature. They'd spent days together without uttering a word. They looked at each other, Buck grinning and looking wise to the ways of nature, Bryce stymied from his stupefaction.

In Ellis's mind a shower came in second best to a full night's sleep. Her first real bath in two weeks revived her well enough for her to work far into the morning before she began to feel the ravages of thirty-six hours without sleep.

It was her heart that compelled her to ask Looty for more work that afternoon, and when the old woman firmly insisted that she take the time off, her mind and body rejoiced. She needed the money, but by noon she was no longer merely dragging her feet; she was plodding to get from one place to the next.

She wasn't sure how she got as far as the LaSalles', but when she turned the old truck onto the half-hidden road leading to the house, she felt pleased that she wasn't going to have to waste the time turning around to look for it.

"Ellis," Anne said, standing in the doorway. "You don't have to knock on the door every time you come home. You live here now." She opened the screen door wide when Ellis appeared not to have the energy, and brought her into the house with one arm around her shoulders. "I put your things in Mrs. LaSalle's old room, second on the left. We haven't redecorated it yet—we wanted to do the nursery first—but the bed works fine, and right now that's all that really counts. You look beat."

She sighed, nodded, and let Anne go on chatting.

"Are you hungry? I could warm up some leftovers, or there's soup."

"Thank ya, but I ate some at Looty's." She smiled feebly at a thought and added, "She makes great biscuits."

Anne growled. "I know. I hear about them all the time. Mine come conveniently out of cans or boxes, and you'd think it was the crime of the century."

"How's Bryce?" she asked, allowing herself to be led up the stairs.

"Aside from a dry hacky cough and feeling drained, he seems fine. I won't ever take an onion for granted again," Anne said with a laugh. "Where did you learn how to do that?"

"The cough is dry, you say?" Her brain was too tired to register more than pertinent facts.

"The cough medicine works great, but when he does cough, he sounds like an old man with pleurisy."

Ellis frowned. "The chest rub should have broken that up."

Anne laughed. "He won't have anything to do with that stuff, and I can't say as I blame him. It makes my eyes water, just to think of it."

"Where is it?" she asked, stopping on the stairs.

"In his room." Anne looked confused and worried and could see that Ellis was in no mood to laugh.

She nodded, turned, and marched up the steps and into Bryce's room like a soldier on a mission.

"I ain't got the time nor the energy to be nursin' the fevers of a childish and ungrateful man," she announced, her arms akimbo as she glared at Bryce.

He was propped up in clean sheets and pillows with a newspaper spread across his lap. He'd been up to shave and shower and to change into a white T-shirt and . . . well, and whatever he had on under the sheets. He looked so handsome, so male, so . . . No! He looked well, she decided, trying to keep her mind on track.

"I see you're as cheerful and easy tempered as ever," he said, grinning at her like a barrel full of possum heads.

Ignoring him and the tingling low in her abdomen, she scanned the room for the mason jar of lard and turpentine she'd mixed that morning. It was standing in a pan of water that at one time had been hot enough to melt the lard.

"I'm goin' down to heat this up again," she told him. "And when I come back you'll be usin' it, or when the poison takes to your head again, I'll let ya die. Ya hear me?"

"There ya go sweet-talkin' me again," he said, unruffled. "I swear, Ellis, if ya don't stop talkin' at me like that, I'm gonna fall head over heels in love with ya."

"You hush," she said, a hand to her midsection to settle a quiet riot of excitement. "Ya wouldn't know beans if ya had your head in the pot. Are ya enjoyin' your poor health?"

"I thought I might, but seein' as how it doesn't bring me any kindliness from my nurse, I'm thinkin' better of it."

"Huh, kindliness," she said disdainfully. "If it's kindliness you want, do as I tell ya and get well. I ain't got the energy to be sittin' up with ya night after night."

She stomped out of the room, down the stairs, and stood tapping her foot in the kitchen while she reheated the rub for his chest, her anger sustaining her. Childish, bull-headed man, she thought. Why was she bothering with him? He was no kin to her. He wasn't a friend. He was a nosy, intruding thief. . . .

She suddenly remembered the pouch of money, still in her coat pocket from the night before. She'd meant to find a proper hiding place for it, but . . .

She hurried down the hall and grabbed her coat from the peg rack near the front door. She squeezed the pockets and sighed with relief when she felt the distinctive bulge of her vast fortune. She frowned, trying to concentrate on the safest place to hide it.

With the ground frozen solid, she couldn't bury it, and with nothing in the world to call her own that was large enough to conceal it, her thoughts automatically turned to the truck. Bryce had found the space behind the loose seat back in the cab, but Ellis was a clever girl.

She was careful to look around for watchful eyes before she peeled back the loose black electrical tape covering a large gaping hole in the seat of the old truck. She removed a goodly amount of the padding, stuffed the pouch in the hole, and then replaced everything as it had been. She pounded the seat three times to restore the indentation that denoted years of wear, well satisfied that her money was safely vaulted away.

"This here's your last chance, Bryce LaSalle," she said a few minutes later, standing at the foot of his bed, the small mason jar of lard in her hands. "You act like a man and use this, or I'm washin' my hands of ya."

She was so tired, she could hardly see straight. Whether he used the rub or not was fast becoming a moot issue.

"Ah, Ellis," he whined, a mischievous twinkle in his eye. "Askin' me to slather that stuff on my body is like askin' me to slit my own wrists. No. Now don't go gettin' all huffy on me again. I don't want ya to be thinkin' that I'm unmanly or ungrateful. I just can't do it to myself, is all." He pushed the sheets low and, pulling the white T-shirt high up on his chest, he added, "But I'd sit quiet and let you do it."

Her eyes lowered to the great expanse of warm golden flesh over tight rippling muscles, then followed the tapering line of coarse black hair to the sheets. She swallowed hard, then met the challenge in his eyes.

She had an urge to shake the tension from her limbs, but stood as stiff as a statue instead. She wanted to laugh hysterically and run away screaming. At the same time, she wanted to look him straight in the eye, do the deed, and walk away untouched. But she couldn't meet his gaze as she inched to the side of the bed and sat down. Her hands trembled when she filled her fingers full of the tepid mixture from the jar and brought them slowly to his chest.

Her fingers tingled with life when she touched him. He sucked in air as if he'd been burnt. She pulled back and glanced up. His gaze met and captured hers in a microsecond. Fire and passion in degrees she'd never seen before flamed within him. Intense, unbearable heat escaped the confines of his body, permeating time and space, scorching her with a stare that held her locked in place, a willing prisoner.

Her heart raced hard and fast; her breathing was ragged and irregular. Her mouth was dry, and her whole body trembled when he took her hand in his and slowly lowered it back to his chest, near the steady pounding of his heart. The muscles in her arms shook as wave after wave of desire and yearning passed from his body to hers and back again, charging her with excitement and a gnawing need deep inside.

He applied pressure to her hand to glide it slowly over his chest. The rub made the passage smooth and easy. He pressed her palm against his hardened nipple, and she watched with fascination as his pupils dilated, unleashing more and more of his passion. She pressed a little harder and grew bolder, like a child playing with matches. She ignited one explosion after another, mesmerized by the bright light, the heat, and the sense of power.

His other hand rose up off the bed. She felt the back of his fingers caress her cheek, gently, tenderly, as if she might break. It was a touch one would use on an object of great worth and enormous value, something precious and adored. It conveyed to her a reverence and admiration, a sense of being cherished. It blocked all thoughts from her mind and brought her senses spiraling freely to the surface of her consciousness.

His touch brought her intense pleasure, and her senses called for more. He stroked her again and again as he might a frightened, skittish animal, soothing and building trust. She closed her eyes and focused on the enjoyment, leaning her cheek into the source.

He traced the outline of her jaw and grazed the sensitive flesh under her chin. Her head lolled loosely to one side, and he drew a path of rapture down the column of her neck, and lower to just above her breasts.

He fanned his fingers, exploring and testing the size and shape of her. Across her shoulder, down her arm, along her thigh to her hip. He discovered her slim waist and fingered her ribs as his hand moved gradually upward, brushing the side of her breast, launching her mind and body into a wild state of cravings and urges.

She took a ragged breath and opened her eyes when his fingers curled about her throat.

"I'm gonna kiss ya, Ellis," he whispered softly.

She might have nodded. She couldn't be sure. She was aware only of the light pressure at the back of her neck and of his features drawing closer and closer to hers, of the consuming light in his eyes and of the urgency she felt. She wanted him to kiss her.

Their lips barely brushed each other. He sampled the taste of her with the tip of his tongue, savored it, indulged himself. Their mouths opened and came together. The flame flared, taunting destiny, provoking the fates, and defying providence. He pulled her tightly to him. Tongues met, one bold and enticing, the other shy and teasing. Passion blazed, and their bodies quickened.

Bryce broke away abruptly, turning his face to cough. When she tried to move away he stopped her.

"No. Stay. Please," he said, the cough short-lived. "Don't leave."

With one arm propped up on the pillow near his head and the other on his chest, she looked down at him, much the way she had the first time she'd seen him—in awe and wonder. She'd seen plenty of men, but none she thought more handsome. She'd been kissed, but never the way Bryce had kissed her. She'd been hungry, but never so ravenous that she ached as she did at that moment.

Bryce tucked a swag of her thick blond hair behind her ear and smiled into her eyes. "Amazin', huh?"

What could she possibly say?

She nodded, lowering her gaze from his to hide the depth of her amazement. She sat up and busied her hands, wiping the turpentine rub off each finger with a towel. Too late she noticed that she'd gotten some on the front of her cotton shirt. Brushing at the stain with the towel, she glanced at him. The quiet, gentle expression on his face shook the foundations of her life.

"Ya couldn't suffer alone?" she asked, hoping to change the look in his eyes, uncomfortable with the emotions she saw in them—even more uncomfortable with the emotions they stirred in her. "Ya had to get this gunk on me too?"

He chuckled.

"You laughin' at me?"

"Yes."

"Well, stop it. This is my best shirt, and ya ruined it. That ain't funny."

"No, it ain't. And I'm real sorry about that. But I ain't sorry we kissed. . . . And you ain't either."

"Who said I was?" She tossed her hair back indignantly and leveled a blue stare at him. It was a gesture she'd used often in the past, daring anyone who saw it to call her bluff. It was foolproof.

"If you're tryin' to pick another fight with me, I won't let ya, Ellis. See, then you could say you were sorry we kissed and you could keep pushin' me away," he said, unperturbed. "But I got your number now, little Miss

Prickly Bush. You ain't so prickly as you'd like me to think."

"I ain't prickly at all," she said, not quite able to hold her stare. She stood to screw the lid back on the mason jar. "Fact is, I think I'm a saint for puttin' up with ya these past days. I shoulda shot ya when I had the chance."

Silence bounced off the walls while they both vividly recalled that she hadn't had a gun to shoot him with in the first place. She turned her head slowly to look over her shoulder at the grin she knew he'd be wearing. A giggle bubbled up in her throat at his wry expression, and they burst into laughter together.

"You're the beatin'est man I ever met," she said, shaking her head in defeat as she lowered herself back to the edge of the bed. Feeling her exhaustion again, she was too weak to fight him any longer.

"Good," he said, well pleased with her, even more pleased with himself. "Assumin' that's your sweetest way of saying ya like me."

She studied him for a moment, pretending deep consideration.

"It's more a way of sayin' that I'm too tired and too confused to keep fightin' with ya," she said finally, stifling a yawn, coming as close as she could to admitting the truth about her feelings.

She started when she felt his hands on her shoulders. He was leaning forward in the bed, directing her back toward him as his fingers began to massage her weary, overtaxed muscles. She whimpered in exquisite discomfort, and he stopped.

"Am I hurtin' ya?"

"No," she murmured in a high-pitched sigh.

His fingers pressed tight muscle against bone, squeezing out the tension and stiffness, circulating a drugging relaxation that went straight to her head. Her eyes closed, her mind faded to a black emptiness, and her spine turned to rubber. Again she whimpered.

"Lay yourself down here," his voice came to her, soft

and coaxing. She was easily turned and rolled face-down into the sheets.

She was vaguely aware of his movements and a faint alarm of danger drifted through a haze of wakefulness when his hands began to knead the pain low in her back and gently grabbed at her thighs and calves. She ignored it. She was perfectly willing to let him kill her with the pleasure and contentment he was inflicting.

He rubbed and massaged her body to a sluglike existence. Her mind drifted through pictures of summer days and autumn evenings, of cold creek water sliding over sand and pebbles, of a golden-haired baby eating daisy petals. And Bryce's face, his eyes twinkling with humor, passion, and gentleness.

"Did ya love her much?" she asked, mumbling into the bedcovers.

"Who?" he asked, his fingers hesitating only a moment.

"Liddy Evans," she said, marginally aware of what she was saying. When he made no immediate comment, she was relieved, thinking that she'd merely thought the question and not really asked it.

"For a while I thought I loved her. I wanted to love her," he said finally, causing a sinking feeling inside her. "But there's a difference between lovin' somebody 'cuz of who they are and lovin' somebody 'cuz they need ya."

It registered in her mind that he had stopped massaging her, but her blissfully numb nerve endings hardly noticed. He stretched out beside her on the bed, his head on a level with hers. He laid flat on his back looking at the ceiling, she remained belly down with her face toward him, refusing to open her eyes.

"It was a lesson I needed to learn about myself. . . . I just wish it hadn't been at Liddy's expense," he said, as if he weren't talking to Ellis, but to himself.

She grimaced, pinching her eyes to keep them shut. She wasn't at all sure she wanted to hear this. She wasn't sure she wanted to get involved in his life, and yet the thought of him with another woman made her unaccountably sad and angry at once.

"I was taken with her 'cuz I thought she needed me," he went on. "And at first she was taken with me for the same reason. There was never anything . . . physical between us. . . . Well, we slept together, of course, but there wasn't any . . . 'lectricity, no sparks, you know? Not like . . ." she heard his head move on the pillow and felt his gaze on her, ". . . not like there should be. And she's got these kids, they're great kids—and I thought they needed me too."

He sighed and went silent for a moment. "I always felt bad 'cuz no one ever seemed to need me as much as I needed them. Growin' up, I mean. It was always Buck and Mama makin' the sacrifices for me . . . and me just . . . growin' up." Again he paused. "They had this plan, Mama and Buck. Buck's smart, see, and he loved school and got good grades. He wanted to go off to college and make somethin' more of himself than just bein' a mill worker. Well, when my daddy died, they hatched this plan to use the insurance money and all their savings to send Buck to college, and then when it came my time to go, he would send me. They had it all worked out. Buck even lied about his age on the papers and got Lenny Watts to go along with him, so he could work a full shift at the mill after school when he was just fifteen. Even my sister donated to the cause. . . ."

"I didn't know ya had a sister," she muttered, her eyes wide open, her heart hanging on every word he uttered. Something in the soft, low tones of his voice had compelled her to look at him and to listen to his story. Pain, sadness, and regret vibrated in the sound of his words, connecting with like emotions inside Ellis, identifying a bond between them, establishing a similarity and closeness between them.

He turned on his side, bringing his nose to within inches of hers, saying, "Brie's her name, it's sort for Brigitte. She's a couple years younger than Buck. She and her husband live in Covington."

"What happened?" she asked, surprising herself with her interest, afraid to admit how avid an interest it was. "Why does Buck still work at the mill?"

"Mama died," he said simply, glancing away briefly. "In a car accident. Buck was off at college. Brie'd just gotten married and moved away. I was seven."

She waited for him to continue. She could tell from the tension in his features that it was difficult for him. She wanted to touch him, to somehow ease his anguish, but she wasn't sure how.

"Buck came home to take care of me. He gave up everything for me."

"And he's been makin' ya pay ever since." How could she have thought that she liked Buck LaSalle, she fumed inside, making an instant reevaluation of his character.

Bryce laughed. "Not Buck. He never said a word. Never treated me any different than before. Never did nothin' but care for me and show me the best way to grow up. He never even got mad when his wife left him 'cuz of me."

"Anne is his second wife?"

He nodded. "He was younger than I am now the first time he got married. Twenty, twenty-one. She never did seem happy 'bout nothing. She complained about the farm bein' too far from town and the house too old. Buck worked too many late hours. . . . She was bored. She was always complainin' about somethin', it seemed, but her favorite and loudest complaint was havin' to put up with me. I was nine or ten by then. She just up and left one day," he said, looking past her shoulder as if watching a replay of the incident on the wall behind her. "Buck always said it was good riddance, but I always thought that they mighta had a better chance of workin' things out if I hadn't been under foot all the time."

"Sounds like good riddance to me," Ellis said, hating the woman and putting Buck back in her good graces.

"Well," he said, reaching out to play with the uneven ends of her thick yellow hair. "Maybe. But my whole life it seemed like someone was givin' up somethin' 'cuz of me. I . . . It bothered me a lot. And I never could find anything to give in return—until Liddy."

Ellis frowned. "What'd she have to do with it?"

"That's just it. She didn't," he said. When she lingered in confusion, he closed his eyes, concentrating on the best way to explain it. "When Reuben first left her, Liddy was a jackpot of need. She was depressed and broke, she had three kids needin' her, and they were lost and confused."

"Lost and confused?" she repeated, knowing a familiar pain in her chest.

"Sure. They didn't know what was happenin'," he said. "But it wasn't Liddy who appealed to me, or the kids. It was them bein' so needy. She was my best shot at givin' back some of what I'd gotten from others. I wanted her and the kids to need me."

"And they did in the beginnin'," he said, mindlessly smoothing her hair from crown to tips, his hand passing onto her back, stroking gently. "I thought I'd died and gone to heaven. I was makin' all sorts of sacrifices, doin' this and that for 'em. I was makin' a real martyr outta myself, 'cuz I knew I didn't love her. The kids are great, and I'm real fond of 'em, but ya gotta love the mother to make a family work . . . and I just didn't. And Liddy . . . well, Liddy wasn't as weak and helpless as she first seemed. She's tough. She just needed time to get herself together."

"What happened?"

"Nothin' really," he said. "We were sittin' across the supper table one night, lookin' at each other, wonderin' what we were doin' together when she didn't need me and we weren't crazy in love or nothin'. So she just said, 'Thanks for the help,' and I left." He shrugged.

"But you're still seein' her, still friends. I . . . I heard ya the other night."

He nodded once. "Reuben is . . ." He frowned, searching for a word that wouldn't offend her ears.

"Low-down?"

"He could wear a top hat and walk under a snake's belly," he said in agreement. "He never was nothin' much, but walkin' out and leavin' Liddy, leavin' his kids like he did . . . It oughta be a hangin' offense."

A hangin' offense. Mental protectors slid into place to protect Ellis's heart.

"Liddy's above his touch, and I think the best thing I ever did for her was to convince her of it, though that wasn't too hard once she was over the shock of his leavin' her in the first place. I gave her money and went with her to the lawyer's office when she filed for divorce, and I drove her back again when she got the restrainin' order to keep Reuben away from her and the kids."

"That's why he's lookin' to hang your hide on the fence?"

"That and me livin' with his wife for six months."

The hand on her back was pacifying to her emotions, lulling her into a state of drowsiness. "You best stay in a crowd after dark," she mumbled, her eyelids closing slowly.

"You ain't worried about me gettin' hurt, now are ya?"

She gave him a disinterested snort. Of course, she was worried about him. In her book, Reuben Evans was a sorry excuse for a human being, the tail end of bad luck, and Bryce was—she felt his light, caring touch on her back—Bryce was the kindest, gentlest, most caring man she'd ever met.

"I hate to tell ya this, Miss Prickly," he said softly. "But ya stink to high heaven."

"So do you," she thought, too beat to speak, obscurely aware of the faint odor of turpentine that filled the air.

"Are ya dreamin', sweet Ellis?" she heard him whisper from afar. She had a one-way ticket to enchantment, traveling in a state of safety and contentment unlike any she'd ever known. "You say ya don't have dreams, only plans. But I'll bet my soul that's as phony as your gun. I'm guessin' that you got plenty of dreams. Mighty sweet dreams." Were those his fingertips on her cheek? So tender and loving? "Look at ya. You're just a sweet dreamin' baby, and that's a fact."

Maybe so, but in all her life she'd never had a dream quite as sweet as Bryce.

Seven

"Howdy, stranger."

"Lord in Heaven!" Ellis complained, her hand over her startled heart, her feet settling on the floor after jumping six feet. "You scared me close to death, Bryce. What are ya doin' here?"

"Well, for two weeks now, we ain't done nothin' but swap howdies at the house. I thought I'd come see how ya were doin'," he said, leaning limply against the storeroom door, unperturbed that she'd turned her back on him and resumed her sweeping.

"I'm doin' fine," she said, her words a bit clipped due to a sudden irregularity in her breathing. She felt as if she'd been running for miles, uphill. Oh, why did he have to make her feel this way, she wondered in quiet misery. Simply hearing his voice made her giddy with happiness; looking at him excited her beyond reason. And yet she dreaded both like a plague from hell.

It had been two weeks since she'd come awake in Bryce's bed, alone and remembering. Every word he'd spoken to her was pressed between the folds of her memory. Some were like wildflowers in a book, unforgettable, treasured, and hauntingly sweet. Some were too painful to be recalled.

She'd slept the afternoon and night away, rising

before the sun, her body revived, her mind as muddled as if she hadn't slept at all.

Bryce was a complication she hadn't planned for when she'd left Stony Hollow to make her fortune; he was a complication she hadn't planned for in her future—ever. She'd had no idea that men like Bryce LaSalle even existed, let alone how to react to him. He confused and delighted her. He distracted her, attracted her like a summer bug to a porch light. He was a row of bad stumps she couldn't afford to tangle with if she wanted to get back to Stony Hollow. And she needed to get back, soon.

He stood quietly at the door watching her, and she did her best to ignore him. Seconds passed. Watching and ignoring came together like invisible waves of hot and cold air, charging the atmosphere with electricity, with lightning and thunder.

"So?" she asked, turning on him when she couldn't stand the tension any longer. "Was there somethin' else ya wanted? I got work to do here."

"I ain't stoppin' ya."

"Well, I can't do nothin' with you standin' there watchin' me."

"Why not?" he asked, a smug look on his face. "Do I make ya nervous?"

"Yes." Why lie? she decided.

"Why do you suppose that is, huh, Ellis?" He tilted his head to one side and looked thoughtful. "You reckon it's the same thing that's kept you skirtin' around me these past weeks?"

"I been busy."

"Too busy to talk to a friend?"

A friend? She'd always been more comfortable with squirrels and raccoons, but the idea of a friend wasn't foreign to her. She'd often wished for a special person to talk to, to laugh with the way she'd seen other people doing. She'd liked telling Bryce about her plans for the future. She'd felt special when he'd told her about his relationship with Liddy Evans. He could make her laugh when he wasn't trying so hard to make her angry, and he had an understanding in him that was deeper and kinder than any she had experienced before. As friends went, she suspected Bryce could be as good as any, and the idea tempted her. Still, she wanted to be honest with him . . .

"I wouldn't know what to do with a friend if I had one," she muttered self-consciously as she bent to sweep dirt and dust into a pan. When he remained silent, she hid behind her pride and turned to face him squarely, saying, "I ain't never had a friend before."

"You got one now," he stated.

His grin was warm and good-natured. In his eyes there was a sincerity and openness that made her want to trust him.

"I never did know what to do with you," she said. "Callin' ya friend ain't goin' to change that."

"May not," he said. "But at least ya won't have to worry that I'll leave ya be when ya tell me to. I ain't ever goin' to leave ya be, Ellis. Friends just don't do that."

She recognized the humor in his expression and responded in kind. "Ya mean they keep comin' around and makin' pests of themselves?"

He grinned. "Yep. That's pretty much it. Good friends can be a real nuisance."

She considered him briefly with narrowed eyes, and in a moment of sheer, unadulterated impulse she decided to do something crazy, to do something she'd always wanted to do—tell a friend a secret.

"Today's my birthday."

She blurted her announcement so abruptly that Bryce wasn't sure what she'd said at first and asked her to repeat it.

"Well," he said, knocked off center a bit. "Happy Birthday. We'll celebrate. Yeah," he exclaimed, finally recognizing the information as an opportunity he should jump on, like a duck on a june bug. "We'll celebrate. Let's see, this makes you twenty-one, right? Lord, you're legal! Now that really calls for a celebration. Tug loves it when someone comes of drinkin' age. Goes all out. Come on, we . . ."

He had her hand and was trying to pull her out of the storeroom when he looked back at her and realized that she'd taken root to the floor.

"Whatsa matter?" he asked.

"We can't tell nobody else."

"Why the hell not? You only turn twenty-one once, Ellis." He took a superior stance. "As your friend, I'm tellin' ya, ya gotta celebrate."

"Maybe next year." He frowned at her. "When I turn twenty-one."

"You're only . . ." His mouth grew lax and his words dwindled as the full significance of her words penetrated his mind.

In the state of Kentucky one had to be twenty to serve hard liquor to the public. They both knew she'd been serving hard liquor for weeks and that Tug Hogan, prizing his liquor license as his livelihood, would see red if he heard of the risk she'd taken at his expense.

It hadn't been the date of her birth that Ellis had given him. She'd just handed him everything he wanted from her. Her faith and her trust. She was as aware as he was that Tug would fire her on the spot if he found out that she'd lied to him.

A smile started someplace deep in his heart and came slowly to his lips.

"Shame on you, Ellis." His grin grew broader when it once again occurred to him that he'd never heard her last name. "Hell, I never had a friend I knew less about than you. What the hell *is* your last name?"

"I use Johnson," she said, feeling incredibly free spirited, sensing that Bryce would keep all her secrets.

She set the broom she'd been gripping against the wall and started for the door. It was time she got back to work. She had two jobs and a friend. What more could a girl ask for on her twentieth birthday? she wondered even as a part of her ached for what she'd left in Stony Hollow.

"You *use* Johnson?" Bryce was asking, thinking her phraseology a bit strange, even for a hillbilly.

She walked ahead of him into the short hall that passed the cooler door and led to the bar. "I never had no proper name till I married Mr. Johnson, and even then I wasn't even too sure it was legal, 'cuz him and the preacher were both drunk at the time."

Still in the storeroom, Bryce stood dazed and looking as if he'd swallowed a rotten pickle. The thought did wiggle across his mind that he'd taken more on his plate than he'd meant to in becoming interested in Ellis, but it was far too late to put any of it back. He liked her too well, wanted her too much, cared about her too fiercely to back away from her now.

"Hey, wait a second," he called, stepping quickly to catch up with her. She had her hand on the door to the bar when he took her arm and turned her toward him. "How come you didn't tell me you were married?"

"It wasn't none—"

"Of my concern. I know. I know," he said, painfully aware that her husband was certainly a concern to him now. "Where is your husband? Does he know where you are?"

She studied him, hesitating to speak.

"Can friends say what's on their mind, even though it ain't the nicest thing to say, and still be friends?" she asked, wanting this new freedom as well.

"'Course. That's the whole idea. Friends know everything about each other," he said, wondering if he'd regret his words later. In the ten minutes they'd officially been friends she'd disclosed a criminal act and a marriage.

She smiled. "In that case, I hope Mr. Johnson is toasting in hell." She paused in amazement. "I shouldn't have said that. It ain't right to speak ill of the dead. . . . But it surely did feel good."

"He's dead?" He felt as if a mountain had been lifted from his chest.

"Devil take him," she said, liking the way it felt to speak her mind and not to encounter a backlash.

Watching her, Bryce chuckled. "You didn't care much for Mr. Johnson."

"Not a tiny bit." She pulled the door open and what had been a muffled noise on the other side became the roar of a boisterous Saturday night crowd.

"How long were you married to him?" he asked, following her. He was on a roll and wanted to know all there was to know about her, afraid she'd clam up on him again.

"Five years."

She said it so matter-of-factly that he had to keep repeating it to put it in perspective. Five years! Mountain girls married young, he knew, but she simply didn't act or look or . . . Lord, he couldn't imagine her having been with another man for so long. Especially a man she hadn't cared for.

He grabbed at a barstool as if he were about to collapse. He sat, his mind whirling with bits and pieces of information until nothing made sense to him.

When he'd touched her, when they'd kissed, he could have sworn she was an innocent, that she wasn't used to being touched by a man, the way a married woman would be. Could he have mistaken shyness for inexperience? Possibly. But he'd kissed a few women in his time, and a man could tell . . . couldn't he?

He watched Ellis carry a tray of beer bottles to a table across the room and tried to imagine her with some man that she didn't like, with any man that . . . well, that wasn't Bryce LaSalle, and nausea churned in his abdomen.

The rage Bryce felt was overpowering and all consuming. Raw and animallike. He wanted her. And in that instant he knew as well as he knew his own name that he'd kill if another man touched her. He went berserk for a minute, picturing himself grabbing a fistful of her thick yellow hair and dragging her back to his cave to protect her and to keep her all to himself.

For a man who was generally easygoing and gentle, it was quite a revelation.

He shuddered and blinked his eyes to clear his head. When he could see straight and think logically again, his gaze sought Ellis—as it did whenever she was around.

She was still across the room, setting the beers on the table one at a time. Perhaps it was the stiff manner in which she moved or the way her head was bent, or maybe it was just that instinct he'd been feeling moments earlier that alerted him to the fact that something was amiss with her. He stood and craned his neck to see who was sitting at the table she was waiting on and what, if anything, was happening.

In the time it took a firefly to light up the night, he was battle ready when he saw Reuben Evans with a sneer on his lips and a taunting glint in his eye, his face turned in Ellis's direction.

"I asked ya a question, girl," Reuben said. Ellis refused to raise her eyes to his and answer. "You dumb or just too stupid to talk?"

"She already told ya she didn't wanna dance with ya, Evans," one of the other men at the table said. "Leave her be. I seen Bryce LaSalle come in a while back. Leave her be."

"I don't care if she's sleepin' with the king of I-ran," Reuben said, grabbing up the beer she'd set before him. "I asked her a question, and I want her answer. These damn hillbillies come driftin' into town lookin' for food and handouts and think the world owes it to 'em. They're livin' off my tax money, so when I ask one a question, I want an answer." He turned his narrow stare on Ellis. "Why won't ya dance with me? Too stupid to dance? Or are ya thinkin' you're too good to dance with the likes of me?"

"Maybe she just don't like your face, man," one of the other men said, laughing, slapping Reuben on the back in a friendly, unoffensive manner.

This wasn't the first time Reuben Evans had come

into the Steel Wheel, gotten drunk, and spent the rest of the night taunting Ellis. Three nights earlier she'd been carrying a tray full of beers to a table near his and he'd tripped her, and though she couldn't prove that it had been intentional, he'd laughed harder than anyone else.

"Don't keep me waitin', hillbilly," he said with a snarl. "You think 'cuz you're sleepin' with a high 'n' mighty LaSalle now that you're more'n just a hillbilly, too good to speak to me?"

"I ain't," she said, looking at him briefly then quickly looking away, afraid of the hatred and anger she saw in his expression. Sleeping with men was something she'd been accused of before. It seemed to go along with being baseborn. But hearing the act coupled with Bryce's name on the lips of Reuben Evans made her ill inside. She set the last bottle on the table and announced the amount of the tab. If he knew how much alike they were, would he still be so hateful toward her? She couldn't help but wonder.

"You ain't what? Sleepin' with LaSalle? Or too good for me?"

She stood stiffly, silently, stoically, waiting for him to pay the bill. It was best to say nothing, she told herself, biting her lower lip to keep it from flapping out words she knew she'd regret. It was best to say nothing, to try and be invisible. He'd tire of his game, she reminded herself. Drunks always got tired.

"Leave her be," the first man said again, nervously. "You're only baitin' her to get to Bryce, and I don't want nothin' to do with it."

"If you're scared of him, go set someplace else," Evans snapped, glaring at the man, who stared back for several seconds before he snatched up his beer and left the table.

Ellis took her opportunity to grab up the money from the table and turn to leave, walking straight into Bryce's arms.

She tilted her head back to look up into his face, but

his gaze was fixed on Reuben Evans—and was as hard and cold as frozen emeralds.

"You got a problem here?" he asked her without looking at her or releasing his hold on her upper arms.

"No," she said automatically, recognizing two men ready to cloud up and rain all over each other. "No problem. Let's go."

She had every confidence that Bryce could hold his own in a fair fight with Reuben Evans, and she felt no guilt in admitting that she'd like to see Bryce clean his plow. But every instinct in her body told her that Bryce wouldn't get a fair fight out of him. He was as mean as a junkyard dog and twice as foul. He was spoiling to harm Bryce in a bad way, and she'd tolerate any abuse rather than see it happen.

"Come on," she said, pushing fruitlessly on his chest. "Let's go."

He continued to stare at Reuben for a long tense moment. He'd drawn a line and was daring the man to spit over it. When he did nothing but stare back, words became necessary.

"If anybody even looks cross-eyed at ya, I wanna hear about it," he said.

The words and the way he spoke them triggered something in Ellis. Her own temper flared up. Who did they think she was? One using her as bait, the other making sounds as if he owned her. She was sick of being used, and she'd die before she let another man own her.

She tore loose of Bryce's hold and left him to glower himself silly at Evans. If they wanted to raise dust, let them, she thought, stalking back to the bar with her tray.

Bryce followed her a few minutes later and tried to talk to her, but she didn't want to have anything to do with him. She'd made another mistake, thinking him a friend.

"What the hell is the matter with you?" he asked, after several attempts to get her attention had failed.

She kept looking through him as if he didn't exist, and it irritated him.

She watched Tug set four beers on her tray and didn't respond. When she left the bar to deliver the beers, Bryce was right behind her, saying, "You never had any trouble speaking your mind to me before. Don't tell me you've gone shy on me."

She stopped at a table in the middle of the room and set the bottles down, unaware that they'd left a trail of turned heads in their wake.

"Dammit, Ellis, I thought we agreed to be friends," he said in a voice that was loud enough to be heard two tables away, above the Patsy Cline record playing in the jukebox. "Friends talk. There can't be any of this cold shoulder stuff. Friends fight fair."

"Well, I told ya I didn't know much about bein' friends," she said, brushing past him, walking toward the bar again. "I sure didn't know they owned ya."

"Owned ya?" He was lost. A woman could get a man lost faster than walking in the woods with a potato sack on his head. It was a fact he knew well.

"Yeah. Owned ya," she said, sending him a querulous glance. "Like ya was a dog or a cow or somethin'."

"What are ya talkin' about?"

Men could be as thick as bricks. It was a fact *she* knew well. Her mouth was full of informative words when she happened to notice that half the people in the bar were watching them. She marched over to the backroom door and passed through, then turned to face him and lay it all out for him.

"I'm talkin' about what ya did out there with Reuben Evans. Makin' like I was a piece of your property," she said, her hands moving to her hips. "I don't need ya to be fightin' my fights for me or struttin' 'round actin' like some rooster defendin' his hen. Folks are already startin' to think we're beddin' down together, and then ya come 'round actin' like I belong to ya. . . . Next thing I know, you'll be smackin' me around just to show 'em that I do."

Bryce was stunned . . . floored . . . out cold, actually. She'd tossed him a few mild punches, then decked him in the final second. He could defend himself against the first few blows, but the last one was a whopper! How could she possibly think . . . ?

"Smack you?" he asked, appalled, hoping he'd misunderstood her. "Smack you? Me?" His voice grew high pitched. "I've never hit a woman in all my life. Not even my sister. Ever. I couldn't. I can't. . . ."

He stopped, slugged in the gut by a sudden streak of insight. He searched her face for testimony to the horror he was feeling, and found it in the depths of her eyes.

He took the pain, fear, and rage he found in her soul and locked it in his heart. Grief and regret stung his eyes, and his hand reached out to her. He palmed her cheek, wishing he could remove the misery delivered by the palm of the last man who had touched her.

"He beat you?" he asked softly, not wanting to believe it, unable to comprehend it. How could anyone, even the world's worst monster, hit a face that looked so like an angel's? "Your husband? He beat you?"

"No," she said, bewildered, rattled by his overwhelming gentleness. "No. He . . . he didn't beat me. He just smacked me around sometimes." As an afterthought she added, "But never when he wasn't drinkin'."

"I'm sorry, Ellis," he said. It was all he could think of to say. He was feeling a multitude of emotions, but his sorrow was the only one he could verbalize. He knew such brutality existed all around him, but he never could abide it.

"No need to be sorry," she said, feeling like a short dog in tall grass about his remorse. Why was *he* sorry? "You ain't laid a finger to me yet, though I been expectin' ya to any number of times."

"Me? I wouldn't. I won't. Ever," he said, a bit disjointed, astonished that she'd think such a thing of him. "Why would I?"

"Well, ya know by now that I have a bit of a temper,"

she said, seriously lamenting her greatest flaw. "And ya musta seen that ya have a real gift for irritatin' it."

He thought *she* had a real gift for understatement.

"I didn't set out to," he said.

She doubted this, but decided to forego comment.

"Well, what it comes to is that I haven't always been able to hold my tongue with you. Mr. Johnson wouldn't stand for my back-talkin'. Not the way you have."

"You thought I'd hit ya for speakin' your mind?"

She shrugged. From the moment she'd met him, she hadn't known how he'd react in any given situation. He was as unpredictable as lightning in a thunderstorm. He laughed when he should have shouted; he was gentle when he should have been angry.

True to form, he surprised her when his other hand mimicked the action of the first, cupping her face. Her breath caught in her throat. He lowered his head and pressed a soft kiss to each cheek before he sipped gently on her lower lip. Her pulse hammered and her body quickened. He nibbled at her upper lip, touched the corners with the tip of his tongue and finally covered her mouth with his.

Her eyes closed slowly but firmly on her old world as a genesis took place within her.

With painstaking care he breathed life into something new and wonderful deep in her soul. An artiste, he created sensations in her body that she'd never dreamed possible. His arms lowered to hold her close in an easy, undemanding embrace. Intuitively she knew she was free to break away. Or to stay if she so chose. She chose to stay.

He awakened a tingling energy that surged through her veins, sensitizing her nerve endings, intensifying his every touch. He delivered her into a state of arousal, alert to the exquisite sensation of pressing her breasts to his chest, aware of the excitement in her midsection, atuned to the pulsating force below that. He was the origin of a new power inside of her and witness to the debut of her sexuality as her hands began to explore the mass and magnitude of his tall, taut body. Her lips grew bold and daring; her body began to tense, impetuously offering him his finest fantasies.

His mouth traveled over her skin, his hands pressed and caressed her body. He pleasured her, giving, demanding nothing in return. Her senses overloaded. She was weak and wobbly. She staggered. Her head reeled when he turned her, placing her back against a solid wall.

His hands returned to her face as if they'd never been elsewhere. His kisses, sweet and tender, tried to wean her back to reality, but she was having none of it. Clinging tightly, she wanted to stay in the wonderworld he'd introduced her to. He pulled his lips away and chuckled knowingly when she whimpered in dismay.

"Do you trust me, Ellis?" he asked, beyond gratified to see passion in her eyes when she opened them.

Trust? He had her in the palm of his hand, defenseless. He could hurt her in any number of ways at that moment, and yet she knew he wouldn't. She knew he'd keep her safe, protect her, treasure her. Did she trust him?

"Yes," she murmured, her voice husky with emotion.

"Then believe that I wouldn't hurt you," he said, wanting her to believe with all his heart . . . wanting her with all his being. He took in the details of her face and suddenly knew, as if he'd been hit in the head with an anvil, that he was falling in love with her. Not because she needed him, but because she didn't need him.

He could have the urge to protect her and he could try to keep her from harm, to provide for her, to do all the things a man was supposed to do for a woman. But he hadn't a suspicion in his brain that there was anything weak about Ellis. Fatherless, motherless, married at fifteen to an abusive husband—Lord knew what else she'd endured in her short life that she hadn't told him about yet—and still she'd emerged spirited, strong, and determined. Ellis could take care of herself. Her life was her own. But just as sure as a cat's got climbing gear, he was going to find a way of convincing her to share it with him.

His hands moved to grip her shoulders.

"If you want to say somethin' to me, say it. Wherever, whenever you got somethin' to say. I wanna know what ya think and what ya feel," he said, his fingers digging into her flesh.

She felt the pressure on her arms but it was miles from painful. Rather, it was a sign of his frank sincerity, and she put her faith in him. 'Course, like ice on a pond, it was always smart to test its strength before venturing too far from shore.

"I want ya to stay away from Reuben Evans," she stated, tensing in anticipation of an explosion.

Surprised, he pulled away from her.

"He's hurtin' you to get to me, Ellis," he said. "This time you're fightin' a fight that ain't yours."

"He ain't hurtin' me. And as long as he's bad-mouthin' me, it is my fight," she said. She hadn't wanted Bryce to come to blows with Evans earlier, fresh from the discovery of his friendship. She surely didn't want them coming together now that she'd uncovered the wondrous feelings a friend could incite in her. Even more selfishly, Reuben was a reminder.

"Ya want me to stand around and let him do that to ya?" He was emotionally, intellectually, and religiously opposed to the idea. Good ol' boys had their ethics, it was part of their charm.

"Yes," she said, but as a pacifier she added, "When he starts bad-mouthin' you, it can be your fight."

Well, there were ways to jump a fence and *ways* to jump a fence, he knew. Reuben Evans was the sort of fence he'd jumped before.

"Fair enough,"he said, a slow grin coming to his lips. "On one condition."

She frowned. "Do friends do that? Put conditions on their word?"

"Sometimes."

In her dreams, friends were friends conclusively, without conditions. But then, she'd found most of her dreams to be silly and unreasonable, which was why she put so little stock in them. Besides, he was standing so close, his eyes were so intense, his lips were so tempting . . . how could she refuse him?

"What condition?"

"Grant me the honor of a birthday dance."

It was an elegant request, and one that flattered her no end, but . . .

"I can't dance." She lowered her eyes. She knew dancing was something a woman ought to know, like plowing and sewing. She'd stolen through the night to sneak a peek at the barn dances back in Stony Hollow more than once. She knew the way of things. Mamas taught their daughters things like dancing and flirting, the way they did cooking and cleaning. Part of Ellis's education had died at birth.

"You can dance," he said, lifting her face to his. "Ya told me yourself you were old enough to do everything but die of old age."

"I meant important stuff. Earnin' a livin', bein' on my own. . . ."

"Important stuff?" He was open mouthed, bug eyed, and looking truly shocked. "Hell, Ellis! There ain't nothin' in the world more important than holdin' a pretty girl in your arms—real close like this—and movin' together to soft music." With a singularly sexy sway of his torso against hers, he demonstrated his point.

Oh my, she thought.

"Ya think if I had me a friend, he could teach me?"

"I think it would pleasure him no end."

Eight

Once, years earlier, Effie Watson had received a box of fancy chocolates from her brother for Christmas. She'd left the box open on the kitchen table, kindly allowing each of the children to take one piece. For Ellis, friendship was just such a gift. For, once she'd taken one piece, she was hard put not to take another.

A curious phenomenon, friendship. It seemed that acquiring one friend entailed the acquisition of several of his closest buddies, which entailed the acquisition of several of their closest companions, which entailed . . . well, Ellis was soon acquainted with half the town of Webster, much to her amazement.

Clear-eyed and cautious as ever, she fostered no delusions as to the cause of her sudden popularity in town. The LaSalles were favored sons in Webster, and it was their stamp of approval that caused the men and women she waited on at the Steel Wheel and at Looty's to lift a hand in greeting when they saw her on the street and to ask about her health in a fashion that made her believe they were genuinely interested.

Still, she wasn't about to turn her back on such amenities. Who would? She liked hearing the sound of a horn tooting in the street, looking up to see someone she knew, and returning their broad smile. She relished feeling welcome and accepted. She reveled in the attention.

"Hellfire and damnation, boy!" Wilbur Jordan complained from his customary place at the end of the bar. "Ya been tryin' to teach that poor little thing to two-step for close to a month now. It's a wonder she can still wait tables the way ya been stompin' on her feet."

It was Saturday afternoon, and the bar was all but empty save the few regulars who came and left early, more interested in catching up on the town gossip than in drinking. Bryce had become one of these regulars, stopping in after work or on Saturday afternoons, using the pretense of giving Ellis another dancing lesson.

He stopped mid-hop, winked at Ellis, then turned a flat expression on Wilbur. "I ain't the one stompin' over here," he said. "I'm the one that's feelin' toes I never knew I had before."

At one time Ellis might have taken offense at his remark, but they had long since come to the unspoken understanding that the exercise was aimed more at facilitating close physical contact than at learning to dance. Besides, she'd already mastered several steps and was growing more confident. . . . More confident about everything, actually.

She'd left Stony Hollow with nothing but the hope that she wouldn't starve to death before she could return. Now she had half the money she needed, work, friends, the knowledge that she could survive outside Stony Hollow, and the freedom to do it.

"If ya think you can do better, old man, be my guest," Bryce said good-naturedly. "No sense in me hobblin' around town by myself. Hope your bones ain't too brittle."

"I'll brittle your bones, boy," Wilbur threatened, chuckling as he slipped off his stool and ambled onto the small dance floor. "What I wanna know is where in hell ya learned all the hoppin' and skippin' ya do? Where'd your people live before they come here? West Virginia?"

Bryce grimaced and wagged his head. "Laugh now, ya ol' coot. You'll be sobbin' in your beer soon enough."

He turned to Ellis, brought her hand to his lips in a Fred Astaire fashion, and kissed it softly. His gaze rose to meet hers, twinkling happily. He grinned at her and her pulse jumped—a reaction she'd come to appreciate and anticipate. He had a way of looking at her that was almost tangible, that touched her like a tender caress, that made her feel like no words could. It made her want to reach out and pull him close to her before he disappeared.

Her muscles tensed in preparation to do just that when he relinquished her hand to Wilbur, saying, "Be gentle with him, Ellis. He's old."

"Peacock," the old gentleman muttered, taking her young hand into his bony one. "I seen Mack trucks turn quarter-ton loads smoother than you turn this little bit o' girl. Ya gotta know how to handle a gal like this," he said, assuming a formal dance position with an affection-filled smirk for his partner. Abruptly, he pulled her smack up against him, saying, "She ain't no high-strung, high-steppin' filly ya can bounce around the floor with. This sweet thing has both feet firmly planted on the ground." He started to shuffle in rhythm to the music, and she followed, too startled to do anything else. "She's earthy and old-fashioned, the way a gal oughta be," he said.

Shuffle, shuffle, step, shuffle, step. He nodded his head once for emphasis, then gave her a toothy grin—minus one or two in front.

Much to Bryce's chagrin, Ellis caught on quickly, and the better she got at the shuffling, the faster Wilbur danced. Before long he was lifting his feet off the floor and had Ellis doing the same until she was dancing the two-step as if she'd been doing it since the first covered wagon topped the mountains.

And she was smiling, a sight that was rare and breathtaking. A sight that was fast becoming as vital to Bryce's existence as his next heartbeat. She was too serious minded, he thought. She worked too hard and worried too much about everything.

Watching her dance, he'd have sold his soul to be able to crawl inside her mind and erase the greater part of her memories, to be able to draw new ones for her—love, happiness, security, contentment.

What got to him most were the times he'd catch her deep in thought with a troubled brow and profound sadness inscribed in the fine lines of her face. It tore him up inside to take a step backward, to remind himself to go slow with her, that she wouldn't appreciate his invasion of her troubles.

Weeks had gone by since they'd first met, and day by day he'd watched her unfold like a prize-winning rosebud. He'd been careful not give her too much heat, had refrained from asking all the questions that plagued his mind. He'd taken pains to water and nurture their relationship, offering not too much and hoping it wasn't too little.

Touching her was the hardest temptation to resist. Her beauty and softness called out to him, the smell of her drove him wild. It was unreasonable to think that touching her would somehow change her perfection, even as tenderly and as sweetly as he wanted to touch her. But in spite of her widowhood, he sensed a purity, an innocence, a certain lack of knowledge in her when they kissed.

Oh, the instincts were there, he thought, shifting his weight uncomfortably against the table on which he sat while she danced with Wilbur, recalling the way she would press herself against him when they kissed, as if she were trying to melt into him. The instincts were there, screaming back and forth between them, wanting and pleading, but still . . .

"Ya see there, boy?" Wilbur called out over the music, a bit winded. "Ain't nothin' to it. She's a natural, she is. And as light as the wind."

Ellis beamed brightly in response to Wilbur's praise.

The old man looked into her face and added, "Prettier than any summer day I ever saw."

He wasn't the only one vying for Ellis's smiles, Bryce noted, pushing himself off the table, feeling a pang of jealousy that he knew was irrational.

"Time to give the wind back to me, ol' man," he said lightly. "Bernice'll skin ya alive if she walks in here and sees ya lookin' at Ellis that way."

"Bernice who?" Wilbur asked, winking broadly at Ellis.

"Your wife?" he said, slipping between the two dancers. "Big woman? Ugly enough to turn a train down a dirt road? Handy with a hatchet?"

"I'm gonna tell her ya said all them things 'bout her, boy," Wilbur threatened, cackling, taking no offense at the description of the woman who'd been his wife for more years than he could remember. "I been tellin' her for years that ya sweet-talk her the way ya do, so's she'll knit ya them fancy huntin' socks ya like."

"Warmest socks I ever owned." He grinned at Ellis, taking Wilbur's warning for the malarkey it was. Bernice Jordan was Webster's official town grandma, charitable, doting, and loved by all. "I'll tell her you're lyin'."

Wilbur walked back to his stool, laughing heartily.

"Bernice ain't a big woman," Ellis said, a frown furrowed between her brows. "And she ain't ugly."

"She knits great socks, though," he said, accepting her lack of humor, taking her into his arms while the records changed in the jukebox. He hand-picked the next one. It was slow, easy, and romantic. His kind of song.

"I gotta work," she said, dodging his grasp. "And ya shouldn't talk ill of Bernice. She's the sweetest—"

He rolled his eyes heavenward and broke in on her tirade. "I was jokin', Ellis. For cryin' out loud! I've known her since I was . . ."

Walking toward the bar, she glanced over her shoulder at him. He saw the grin and the teasing sparkle in her eyes and knew the joke was on him. There was hope for her yet, he decided with growing regard.

"Gettin' real smart, ain't ya?" he said, trying hard not to smile as he followed her off the floor.

"Yes, sir, I am," she said, acting cocky. "Smart about you, anyway."

"What's that mean?" He settled himself on a stool, rubbernecking to see her face as she bent over the sink behind the bar, washing empty beer glasses. "What's that mean? Smart about me?"

"You're a flirt."

"Me?" He was going to deny it but thought better of it. "Well, maybe I do a little."

"A little? You sweet-talk every woman to cross your path. Looty. Bernice. Anne. Me. Poor Mrs. Elliot down at the fillin' station. Lord knows who else."

"I don't flirt with Anne. Buck'd kill me," he said, lying to see her reaction.

She was flabbergasted.

"Are ya even goin' to deny that ya flirt with me?" she asked.

"I do flirt with you. I flirt with all the ladies I want somethin' from. It's part of my charm."

Her eyes narrowed suspiciously. "What are ya tryin' to charm from me?"

His grin was slow and mischievous. He looked at her in a way he had that aroused the jitterbugs in her stomach and sent her heart skipping about in her chest.

"My mama used to tell me it wasn't polite to ask for candy," he said. "She said it was better to wait until it was offered to me."

She had a feeling that there was a deeper meaning to his words, and that whatever it was was going to make her feel awkward and uneasy if she pursued it, so she changed the subject.

"You do flirt with Anne," she said. "She told me so."

"Never."

She took on a scornful expression. "Not even the night ya asked her to take me in?"

Taken back, he swallowed hard and had the grace to look sheepish. "That . . . was . . . closer to begging than flirting," he said, wondering what she was going to do now that she knew she'd been tricked. "How long have you known?"

"A few weeks."

And she was still speaking to him? he thought.

"I came home from work and caught her haulin' wood in from the shed," she explained when he continued to stare at her in a stunned silence. "She musta lost track of the time, 'cuz she'd forgotten to hide all the laundry she'd toted up and down the stairs. I'd been thinkin' there was a mite less of it than there oughta be for four people."

"What'd she say?"

"Said you came knocking on her door in the middle of the night, asking her to take in a girl ya'd met in the bar that night."

"I think I asked her to take in a *pretty* girl I'd met in the bar," he interjected, teasing her, hoping to charm his way out of a heavy punishment.

Ellis wasn't buying it. "When she didn't cotton to the idea of takin' in a stranger that no one ever saw before, she said ya flirted with her and sweet-talked her into sayin' yes."

He could see that his best defense would have to be a good offense. "Flirted and sweet-talked her? That's what she said?" She nodded. "Well that ain't true. I begged like a dog and promised to do her share of the dishes for the rest of my life."

Laughter bubbled up and out of Ellis like soapsuds in a long-necked bottle. He was the beatin'est man! she thought, and Lord above, she loved him because of it. . . .

Sobering, she looked at him, looked at him through new eyes, as if seeing him for the first time. Did she love him?

Love was something she knew about. She knew what it was to have it and what it was to be without it. It was the best and the worst of all emotions. It was incredibly wonderful and excruciatingly painful, a blessing and a curse, something to die for and the only thing that made life worth living.

But did she love Bryce? All she knew was that if he turned his back on her and walked away, he'd take a huge part of her with him—a part of her that she had denied too long, thinking it unimportant. A piece of her that needed confirmation—her self-worth, her intelligence, her identity.

Her life had been a constant struggle against degradation and despair. Born into a state of disgrace, she'd grown up in shame. There was no one but herself to believe that her life had value, that she was good and that there was a purpose to her existence. Some days she hadn't believed it herself. Some days it hadn't mattered. . . .

It mattered to Bryce. His respect and consideration reaffirmed her faith in herself, echoed and strengthened her opinion of who she was. His gentleness nurtured hope and encouragement. His decency, warmth, and his own sense of significance had a grip on her spirit, heart, and mind. He had become an integral part of them.

"Ya really promised to do Anne's dishes 'cuz of me?" she asked, marveling at her emotions.

"I begged too." A greater sacrifice, in his opinion. He kept his head pitifully bent, toyed with a near-empty beer bottle, and gave her plenty of time to feel guilty and remorse and respond with an appropriate amount of gratitude.

When she didn't respond at all, he glanced up at her. A queer sort of tenderness had taken control of her features, and a familiar glint in her eyes made his pulse jump. His muscles flexed automatically. He'd seen that glint at least seventy-five . . . maybe a hundred times since he'd grown his first moustache. A cold sweat broke out over his body. He lowered his gaze from hers, then scanned the room to see if anyone else had noticed the bold message written on her face.

"Ya ain't mad." She'd given him five acres of hell for doing less than lying to her. "How come?"

"Anne said I shouldn't be," she said simply with a shrug. She slipped the empty bottle from his hand and tossed it away, using her expression to ask if he wanted another. When he shook his head, she continued, "She said ya done her a favor, that she hadn't known how . . . ah, how . . . insecure she'd felt bein' pregnant and on the other side of the mountain without another woman 'round for miles. I give her peace of mind, she said."

She wasn't giving any to Bryce, however. She leaned casually back against the cooler door, hooked her thumbs in the pockets of her jeans, and splayed her fingers across her abdomen, unwittingly drawing specific attention to that general area of her body. His muscles knotted in chaotic excitement. He squirmed nervously on the stool and shifted his eyes back to hers—not that it helped.

"'Course, I've a notion she was just being nice," she said, unaware of the effect she was having on him. "She's a right fine person, but I told her I couldn't stay. Havin' a woman's body don't mean I eat any less, ya know. So we agreed on the chores I was to do, and then . . ." she hesitated, recalling the moment warmly, "then we had tea together at the kitchen table and talked. I never done that before."

"What? Had tea?"

"No. Set with another woman, just to talk."

He groaned. "Girl talk. I won't ask what ya talked about."

"You mostly," she offered the topic anyway, smiling slyly.

For a split second he thought he might break out in a blush. He willed himself to stay cool and smile back. "Musta been a short back and forth."

"A good hour or more is closer to it."

He cleared his throat, as apprehensive as a frog with a busted jumper on a busy road. He went hot and cold in spurts. Hellfire! Was he losing his mind? he wondered. They finally agreed on something, and he was acting like a jackass. She wanted him, he knew the look. And he wanted her. How much simpler did it have to get?

"I'd best be gettin' back," he said, wanting to kick himself.

If any other female had looked at him the way Ellis was, he'd have waited out her shift and asked her to the movies. He'd have kissed her silly in the balcony, and then jumped her bones before they made it back to her front door. What was he waiting for?

"Are ya still workin' on the cupboards in the kitchen?" she asked, knowing he spent most of his free time working on his house—free time, that is, that he didn't spend at the Steel Wheel with her.

"Yep. Should have 'em finished soon," he said, patting his body, searching for his pockets as if he'd lost them. He pulled out a five-dollar bill and laid it on the counter. "Are ya workin' later tonight?"

She took the five and made change for the single beer he'd sipped on. Not for the first time did she realize that he wasn't much of a drinker. She sighed happily.

"That a yes or a no?" he asked, watching her closely.

"What?" My oh my. What a dither she was in—and wasn't it wondrous?

"Are ya workin' late?"

"Ah . . . no. Tug don't need me," she said, recalling that she hadn't been pleased with the news. Saturday nights were money in her pocket, and she wished she could work them all. . . . But there was a bright side. "Maybe after supper, you could show me your cupboards."

Her Saturday night off meant he wouldn't have to make another trip to town, wouldn't have to spend the night in the bar waiting for Reuben Evans to make an appearance and hopefully a wrong move, wouldn't have to be near her in his present state of confusion. . . .

"Sure. Anytime," he said before he could think of a way to put her off. "I'll see ya later."

Ellis watched him leave.

When a girl grew up to be a woman, there were things she knew. Womanly things that needed to be heeded. Well . . . Ellis was a woman and she was paying heed to them.

Effie used to tell her that God sent every bird its food, but He didn't throw it into the nest. Well . . . Ellis knew what she wanted. She knew what she needed. And she knew how to go out and get it.

Nine

Bryce had never been the dreamer his older brother was. He didn't want to be anyone important, didn't want to be a crusader or save the world. Big cars, overblown houses and a cushy bank account had long ago fallen low on his list of priorities when compared to deer hunting on a chilly fall morning, fishing in the summertime, or lying in a field of tall grass and sucking in the clear, sweet Kentucky air while he watched the clouds push each other across a bluer than blue sky.

Anne called him earthy, he called himself smart. He was only going to get one life, and he wanted to take his time and enjoy every second of it. To his way of thinking, God wouldn't have created trees and water and sunshine if he had wanted a body to work in an office all day.

A man didn't truly own many things during his lifetime. Fewer still were the things he could say he was genuinely proud of accomplishing. But when he came to the bottom of it all, a man was a veritable king if he was lucky enough to love, be loved, and fit in somewhere.

"Ain't nothin' fancy," Bryce said, surveying the unpainted drywall and bare floors that represented a dozen smashed fingers, a bathtub full of sweat, and more loving care than he'd ever invested in an inert object before. The house was a place of his own, a place where he belonged, that belonged to him—and he was surprised at how much he wanted Ellis to like it. "It'll keep the rain and the wind out, though, and buildin' it with my own two hand'sll give me somethin' to boast about when I'm an old man."

She smiled at him, but he didn't see. Actually, he hadn't looked at her more than six times all evening. He'd been restless throughout dinner, jumping when spoken to, fiddling with but not eating his food, quiet and introspective in a way that worried Ellis. And then he'd left.

She'd bided her time, clearing the table and wistfully watching as Annie joined Buck at the sink to dry the dishes he washed, which she did frequently, as if any opportunity to stand beside her husband, to share any task with him, to talk softly with him was golden and not to be missed.

She had left them to their time together and crept upstairs to her room.

In her clear-thinking, deliberate, Ellis-like fashion, she removed the clothes she'd worked in all day and set out a nearly identical set that was clean. She didn't waste more than a minute or two wishing her underwear was the low-cut, flimsy sort she'd seen in catalogs before she changed into a fresh set made of sturdy cotton.

Dressed, she brushed her hair and pinched her pale cheeks so she wouldn't look as nervous as she was beginning to feel.

The birds Effie had told her about gathered their food using only the instincts the good Lord gave them. Ellis was praying that He'd given her equally keen senses to reap what she needed.

Bryce had left his porch light burning—she took it as a good sign. He greeted her at the door with a smile, and she was encouraged. But the situation went downhill after that.

He was cordial and talkative, showed her the cupboards he'd been working on and several other new additions he'd made since her last visit, but he was as fidgety as a cricket in a hot skillet. She followed him from room to room and watched as he turned on lights, fiddled with this, moved that, and dillydallied with something else—hardly looking at her and making it absolutely impossible to get within three feet of him. What was she doing wrong?

"You don't need to wait till you're an old man, Bryce," she said, her voice soft with uncertainty. "Ya can boast all ya want now. Ya've done a fine job. It's a grand house."

"Ya think so?" His glance flicked her way.

"I do. I'd be proud to call it mine."

"Ya would?" Hellfire! He'd made snappier conversation as a twelve-year-old!

"It's finer than any house I ever saw, 'cept Mr. Johnson's," she said, and then not wanting to detract from the compliment she added, "But his was old, and if it ever held any happiness in it, I never seen it."

Bryce looked at her then, a puzzled frown on his face, his eyes watchful.

"How come ya married that guy?" he asked after a few seconds of mental debate. He wasn't sure he wanted to know, and he was positive that it wasn't any of his business. Her yesterdays were hers. All he wanted was her today, every day for the rest of her life. "Why didn't ya go back to livin' with the old lady ya told me about?"

Granny Yeager. Ellis had gone higher up on the mountainside and deeper into the woods to live with Granny Yeager after Effie Watson had died. The old woman had outlived her entire family and had a hankering to give up the ghost herself—except that she couldn't seem to die at will. She'd taken Ellis in as a favor to Effie, who for many years had been the only soul who'd visit the reclusive old woman.

Granny Yeager had the power. She could heal anything that bled, and what didn't she ate. Most folks were afraid of her, including Ellis at first. But like those who came to the widow in desperation and fear of losing a loved one, Ellis, too, had found it impossible not to believe in her.

In the three years they spent together, it was Ellis's considered estimation that they spoke fifty words to each another. Still, the woman had fed her, clothed her, kept her warm, and taught her a thousand miracles of nature—including the ones she'd used to break Bryce's fever and cure his cough.

All in all Ellis looked back on those years as being not so bad. She wasn't loved as she had been by Effie, but then she wasn't looked down upon or belittled in those years either.

When she was fourteen, Harlan Johnson had come to Granny's cabin asking for help. His wife was dying, and he didn't know how best to tend her.

Granny, old and set in her ways, was willing to send potions and give verbal instructions, but she wasn't about to leave her cabin for long. When Mr. Johnson pleaded with her, giving no indication of going away until he got what he wanted, she offered Ellis's services, assuring him that she knew enough to tend his wife.

"Granny Yeager didn't want me back," Ellis said simply, feeling no malice toward the old woman. "She told me when I left. I was fourteen. I could hunt and fish as well as she could. I could cook and plow and tend the weak. It was time for me to make my own way."

Bryce looked angry for a moment, opened his mouth to say something, thought better of it, and remained silent.

He reined back his temper, and in a voice that barely hid it asked, "Why didn't you? Ya coulda left Johnson's house once the wife died, right? Why'd ya stay?"

She waited to speak, vacillating between the truth and anything she could make up quickly that would hold water later.

The truth . . .

"I was afraid," she murmured, lowering her eyes to an

unseen spot on the floor. When he didn't speak, and she couldn't stand not seeing his reaction, she looked up at him. His face held no expression. No anger, disappointment, or pity. Nothing. He just stood there, across the room, looking at her.

"I wasn't happy there," she said, the words bursting forth in her need to make him understand and not think less of her. "I wanted to leave. I was plannin' to. . . . I . . . In the things Effie saved for me—the things that were my mama's? There was a letter to her from her mama. I . . . used to read it. Over and over. She sounded like a fine woman, like . . . like I used to think my mama was. I used to . . ." She looked upward as if seeking the courage to admit her most grievous sin. "I used to dream about writin' to 'em one day. See, in this dream I had, I always figured they didn't know 'bout me, that maybe my mama forgot to write and tell 'em, or maybe she was keepin' me for a surprise. . . ." Her dreams sounded insane when spoken aloud. She went silent.

"Ya wrote 'em," he said, knowing her well. She nodded, her eyes downcast. "What happened, Ellis?"

"They didn't want me neither," she said, her voice a bare whisper squeezing past the lump in her throat. "They sent me back a hateful letter, telling me I was doin' a . . . a cruel trick on 'em."

"So you stayed with Johnson."

She walked aimlessly beside the counter as if inspecting it, unable to stand still any longer and incapable of meeting his gaze.

"He talked to me about it, even before his wife passed on. He said he'd be needin' a body to keep the house and tend his family. He said that he didn't think he could rightly keep me, once his wife was gone, if he didn't make me his legal wife," she said, pausing, wondering how much of her married life she should tell him about. "I put him off for a while, hopin' my mama's people would . . ." She shrugged. "But then it didn't

seem like I had much choice. I . . . I was afraid I'd
starve to death or . . . or die in the cold. I—"

Suddenly she couldn't breathe, crushed in a bearlike
hug with her nose pressed tightly against Bryce's chest.

"I want ya, Ellis. And I won't let ya starve or die in the
cold. I won't let ya be lonely or sad. I won't let anyone
hurt you ever again." He took her face in his hand and
said, "I don't want ya to leave me, Ellis. I want this to be
your home. And I want ya to let me share it with ya."

He covered her mouth with his and kissed her hard,
long, and thoroughly. He gasped for air and was about
to do it again when he felt her lips moving against his,
saying, "I reckon havin' a baby ain't so bad, compared
to goin' insane."

"What?" he asked, his eyes still closed, his mouth
still eager to join with hers.

"My plans," she murmured, her lips tickling his. "I
wasn't plannin' on havin' a baby, but I can't take no
more of this."

His head came back, and he frowned at her. "What
are you talkin' about?"

She frowned back at him. "Babies."

"Well? What about 'em?"

"Well, I wasn't planning on havin' none for a while, if
ever. I . . ." She was about to tell him why, when he
interrupted, a bit surprised and very amused.

"Well, I wasn't plannin' on havin' any right this
minute either," he said, chuckling. "And we don't need
to talk about 'if ever' right this second, do we?"

She groaned in misery and let her forehead fall
dejectedly to his chest.

"I can't take no more of this," she complained. Effie
had been right. Womanly urges were overpowering.
They made her feel weak all over and were threatening
to consume her mind in total darkness. "I got the
commotion inside my body. I'll go insane for sure if I
can't have ya."

He laughed and pulled her close. "I know the commotion. I got it myself." He raised her face to meet his. He kissed her. "I'm yours for the askin'."

"Now."

He grinned with joy at her impatience.

"You run upstairs, and I'll turn some of these lights off down here," he said, turning her toward the railless staircase and his bedroom on the second floor. He placed a string of kisses along the back of her neck, and when he felt her limbs go loose and jerky, he whispered in her ear. "I bet I can turn out all the lights and still beat ya to the bed."

He chuckled when she simply nodded and shuffled off. He didn't wait to watch her, but enthusiastically set about his task. In semidarkness, with a single light at the top of the stairs to guide him, he bounded up the steps two at a time and into his bedroom. He stopped cold at the door.

The light shown in on Ellis. She was stretched out on the bed, fully clothed except for her boots, and laid out . . . hell, like one of those sacrificial maidens he'd seen in books. Stiff, stoic, prepared for the slaughter—not exactly the zealous lover he'd been expecting.

"Ellis?" She turned her head to look at him. "You okay?" He saw her slight nod. "Nothin's wrong?"

"You're takin' a bit too long, is all."

Her bold words came out on a tremor of nerves and made him wary. He crossed to the bed and looked down at her. It was too dark to see into her eyes, and the rest of her face showed no signs of stress, only its soft smooth lines, the curve of her chin, and her sweet, sweet mouth.

He sat on the edge of the bed and reached out for her. He jumped back startled. She was as rigid and hard as stone.

"For crissake, Ellis, what's wrong with you?" he asked, gruff in his concern. He felt instant regret, and in a softer tone he asked, "Are ya scared of me?"

"No."

"Well, then . . ." This could get tricky. What if she

thought younger men were bigger than older men? Or more aggressive, more ferocious in their lovemaking? And were they? he wondered, feeling incredibly warm all of a sudden. ". . . are ya afraid I'll hurt ya?"

She answered with a slow, "No."

"Can ya tell me what's botherin' ya, Ellis?"

"Ain't nothin' botherin' me," she said, growing testy with his delay. "I'm waitin' for ya to get at it."

At what? The sacrificial ceremony? He sat for a minute to ponder the situation, then finally got up and turned on the lights.

"I think we should have a little talk before . . . I get at it," he said, none too sure of himself. He'd never had to explore a woman's sexual history before or, heaven forbid, explain the act to her.

She groaned, chafing with intolerance. There she was, freely offering herself to a man for the first time, and he wanted to talk!

He sat beside her once more. His palms were sweating, and his mouth felt as if it were stuffed full of cotton. "I wanna . . ." He cleared his throat. "I need to know how it was with you and . . . Johnson. You and your husband." Lord, he thought he'd never get it said. "Did he . . . Did he hurt you?"

"Just the one time," she said, taking a closer look at him. Seeing his worry and distress, her frustration shifted toward curiosity.

"Which time?" he asked, filled with dread.

"That one time."

"Which one?"

"The only one."

She could have hit him in the face with a bag full of stones, and he wouldn't have been more floored.

"In five years? He only had you once in five years?" He stared at her in disbelief. How could anyone resist her that long?

"Only 'cuz he had to ."

"What?"

"Well, he had to make the marriage legal, didn't he?"

She was beginning to wonder if he was acting stupid on purpose. Was he stonewalling her? Didn't he want her the way she wanted him? "It was frightenin', and it hurt like the dickens for a while after he left, but once he got at it, it was over soon enough and he never did it again, not even . . ."

"What? Not even what?"

"He'd been drinkin' that night, and sometimes . . . when he was drinkin' he'd look at me weird, like he hated me more'n usual, like he wanted to hurt me again. I took to hidin' when he started drinkin', but he never did come lookin' for me again."

"Never . . . again." It wasn't sinking in.

"I told ya. He only married me in the first place so I could stay in his house and tend him without every livin' mother in the hollow ayakkin' 'bout it. He didn't want me for bearin' children, just for doin' chores. He had sons that were grown and married already."

"There were two, right? And they all lived together," he recalled from previous discussions. "They needed three women to care for the house? How big was it?"

"Little bigger than your other one. Anne and Buck's place," she said, coming to a sitting position when she realized their little talk was going to take a while. "But Jewel and Patty—the other Mrs. Johnsons besides me—they always acted like they were born tired and never got rested. They just sorta followed the shade 'round the house and left the chores to me."

The picture of her marriage to Harlan Johnson was developing a little too clearly for him. Bryce didn't want to hear anymore. He wanted to love her so hard and so long that her years in the Johnson house would seem a five-second nightmare, done and gone. Trouble was, he *needed* to hear more.

"That night, Ellis, the one night . . . Can you tell me what happened?"

"What happened?" she asked, thinking it a queer question from a man who had an outstanding reputation with the ladies of Webster—if bathroom gossip was any indicator. She shrugged uncertainly, saying, "What always happens, I guess."

"Did he kiss you?"

"No. Not like you do," she said, trying to remember a dull, faded memory. "He smelled somethin' fierce, so I kept my face turned away. He slobbered on my neck a bit, but he was pretty loaded, it might not of been a kiss. Why are ya askin' all these questions?"

He studied her angel face, her clear blue eyes, and saw only her innocence and purity. She was a virgin-widow. Harlan Johnson had touched her body, but not her heart or her soul. Whatever the old man had done to her that night so long ago, she had perceived as a natural act in her mind. It had been unpleasant, even painful, but he had presented it to her as something expected of her, of all married women. He'd left her with misconceptions, not emotional scars.

Suddenly inspired, Bryce grinned at her.

"Let's try a new angle on this," he said. Showing was always better than telling. And seeing was believing.

"What?" she eyed him suspiciously, frowning at his strange behavior. Though she didn't know why she was frowning—his behavior was strange to her a great deal of the time. "What kinda new angle?"

He laughed softly as he stood and extended his hand to her.

"You laughin' at me again?" she asked, ready to feel hurt and insulted.

"No." Taking her hand, he brought her to stand before him. "I'm laughin' 'cuz you're in for a *big* surprise." Holding both her hands, he shook the still tense muscles in her arms. "Relax."

"I don't like surprises, Bryce."

"You'll like this one," he said. "I promise. And all you have to do is relax and trust me. Can you do that?"

She was dubious. "I'll try."

"That's my Ellis," he said, his voice low and throaty as he slid his fingers along her neck and into her hair, lifting her face to his. Without a shred of fear in them, her eyes closed. His lips grazed hers.

She pulled back suddenly. "We're gonna do it standin' upright?"

Green eyes met blue. His smile was debonair. "We're goin' to do it standin' up and layin' down. Hell, before we're done, we might do it upside down. Just tell me what ya like best. This . . ." He kissed her neck below her ear and littered several more along her throat while he released the first two buttons on her cotton shirt. Dropping kisses low inside the opening, he asked, ". . . or this?"

"Yes," she whispered, her breath short and gaspy. She liked it all. His every touch hit her like a brick of utter delight. Wild tickling sensations ran amok through her body, gathering and multiplying in her breasts.

"Good," he said. "What about this . . ." He opened his mouth over hers, plundering with his tongue, teasing and enticing. He pulled the tail of her shirt from the waistband of her jeans and pinched the rest of the buttons free. He lifted his head and waited for her to look at him.

The passion in his eyes was heart-stopping. Air caught in her throat like a solid object. Mesmerized by the strength of his desire, in awe of the potency of her own emotions, she lowered her eyes and simply watched as he pushed her blouse back over her shoulders.

". . . and this?" he murmured, his hands at her bra straps, stretching them low on her arms before he bent to taste the lush valley between her breasts again and again.

Her eyes were glazed with yearning; her lips were wet, kiss-swollen, ready to be taken again; her bare chest heaved with excitement.

He wanted to teach her about lovemaking. Not just the sexual act, but more. The careful building of trust and devotion. The painstaking construction of a relationship between two people that would endure until the end of eternity.

The hollow gap in his life, the hole he'd tried to fill with stray dogs, Liddy Evans, and every down-and-outer to come his way, closed. She filled the emptiness in his life. He had something to give her, something she couldn't give to herself, something she couldn't buy, borrow, or barter for. He'd been given more love in his life than he'd ever known what to do with. And now he could give it to her.

He held her closer than close, kissing her deeply, pouring every drop of the devotion he felt into her soul as a source of power she could always rely on and never doubt; into her heart to heal the wounds left by those who were blind to her goodness, her pride, and her unflagging character; into her body to drive her senses beyond her control, leaving her exposed and defenseless . . . but only to him.

The teacher in him smiled when he felt her hands move across his shoulders and down his back, searching and exploring. As the master shares his secrets with the novice, he led the way, peeling her clothes away, caressing, savoring every inch of pale warm flesh he uncovered.

Like a sorcerer, he cast a spell over his apprentice. Her head reeled. Time and space merged in a cloud of mystical ecstasy. A power, unseen and unheard but felt in every fiber of her being, took possession of her. She grew bold, brave, and brazen. Her hands trembled with its energy as she tore at his clothing, grappling with buttons and cloth in her haste to absorb more of his great wisdom.

He presented her with a tall, lean masculine form for experimentation. Corded sinew bulged mightily under smooth skin. It was warm and titillating to touch, to stroke, to taste. She grew heady with her newfound ability to interfere with the tight control he was exerting on his body, to feel the muscles jump and tighten under her fingertips, to hear him suck in a deep breath and release it in a spasm of pleasure. Her hands and eyes wandered freely, wherever they took a notion to go.

An insatiable hunger for knowledge soon filled her mind and weakened her body. She leaned heavily against him, panting, amazed by the way their hearts hammered together in syncopation. Cold sheets soothed her feverish skin. Dim thoughts came and went without significance. Suddenly she was missing him.

"Bryce?" she called, her voice sounding far away. She opened her eyes and felt the mattress sag under his weight at the same time.

"Shh," he whispered, nuzzling her neck, palming a path from between her breasts to the top of her thigh. "I'm here."

"What . . ."

"Shh . . ." He silenced her with his mouth, and having anticipated her question sometime back, answered when he could. "We won't be makin' any babies tonight."

"No? But . . ."

"They ain't part of the plan just yet." He suckled her breast selfishly, tilting out of focus when a soft moan of pleasure escaped her.

Slowly, meticulously, he imparted all his best techniques and formulas—she was an excellent pupil. He wanted to take his time, show and experience everything with her. Her wonder made it all new and fresh for him. Her reactions moved him, drove his endurance to the breaking point.

Cautiously, as if she'd never been taken before, he eased himself into her and was gratified beyond words when, frenzied, she impaled herself, her hands on his buttocks pulling him closer, deeper. Together they crossed over the fragile margin between body and spirit, between exquisite torment and bliss.

She lay breathless and exhausted, aware only of the slowing of his respirations and the steady thumping of his heart beneath her cheek. Bit by bit, as if awaking from a night of sweet, tender dreams, her world readjusted itself. Her past swept past her in a flash of gloom and sadness, and her arms automatically tightened around Bryce.

He held her close, responding to the pressure of her embrace, sensing her reluctance to terminate their intimacy, feeling a sad reluctance of his own.

"Whoa! What's this?" he asked, looking from the tear on his arm to those in her eyes and on her cheeks. She quickly turned her face away, and when he would have turned it back to him with a caring hand, she made a nose dive under the covers.

"Don't look at me! And don't ya dare laugh!" she mumbled furiously, angry with her behavior, flustered with her futile efforts to stop the tears. "And cut off the gall-darned light. Oh!" she wailed miserably. "I'm actin' like a baby. I don't wanna . . . I can't make 'em stop." The bed bounced once and then again when semidarkness shrouded her in privacy. She could feel him next to her, not invading, but waiting. "None of your other women cried, I bet. I hate whiny, weepin' women, don't you?" She sniffed loudly. "I . . . I never cry, never." She cried softly into the sheets for several minutes, and when she tired, she muttered, "I didn't know."

Her weeping hurt. It left him feeling unmanly and helpless, but he let her cry anyway. In his bones he knew it was a tempest that had come a great distance and lingered on the horizon for far too long.

"I didn't know," she said again, bewildered.

"What didn't ya know?" he asked, his voice gentle and undemanding.

"That it could be like this," she muttered. "I didn't know anything could be like that. Nobody told me."

"Maybe nobody knew. It ain't like that for everybody," he said.

"The first time . . ." The covers moved. "He hurt me."

"He didn't love or care about ya, Ellis. It was just somethin' he had to do. It didn't mean nothin' to him. And it shouldn't mean anything to you either. Forget it," he said, stroking the sheet that covered her arm, trying to ease the pain of her memories.

Forgetting wasn't that easy. Her whole life had changed that night; it was the foundation on which she'd built a life for herself and for . . .

"I need to tell ya somethin'," she said.

It was time. She didn't want anything between them. No lies. No hidden truths. There were things about her Bryce needed to know. And if he hated her? It was a chance she'd have to take.

"Then uncover your face and tell me."

She hesitated. "If you're grinnin' like a fool and thinkin' to tease me, I'll slap ya so hard your lips'll stick to the wall," she warned him. "I ain't in no mood for your nonsense, Bryce. This is important."

"Sober as a judge, I promise."

Flicking back the sheet, she saw him grave and unsmiling, but he didn't give her a chance to speak. He pressed his mouth to hers in a kiss that was warm and caring and ever so tender.

"Let's talk later," he whispered near her ear. "All I wanna do right now is love ya." Their lips touched softly.

"There's things ya gotta know about me. . . ."

"No." His kiss was hard with passion and deep with faith. "All I still need to know is whether or not ya love me too."

"I do," she said, wrapping her arms around his neck, aligning her body with his. "I do love you."

Maybe it wasn't the time to tell him, she mused, her mind and body slipping into a land of sensational magic; her need to be loved overpowering her compulsion to be honest with Bryce. Maybe after she had the money and after she returned to Stony Hollow to rectify her life, perhaps he would understand better, perhaps he would think less harshly of her. . . .

Ten

Winter stomped through the mountains of Kentucky. It was cold as kraut—pinchy, biting cold. Snow fell as thick as a featherbed, and each morning was fresher than the morning before. Raw, windy, and a whole overcoat colder.

Yet Ellis thrived. Warm, well fed, and well loved, she took a new look at the world and grew optimistic about the future. She'd never doubted her ability to work hard for what she wanted, but with Bryce at her side the burden of failure was less ponderous. She wallowed in his love and allowed herself to believe in the dreams she'd once discarded as impossibilities.

Opportunities came and went for her to tell Bryce about her last five years in Stony Hollow. As he was content to be living in the present with her and doing everything in his power to help her forget her past, she was even more firmly set in her mind that once she could make her life right and whole again, he would better understand her actions—for both, it was one day at a time, scratching only where it itched.

Thanksgiving arrived in a flurry of snow, and even though Looty offered her the day off, Ellis chose to work it.

Every year Looty opened her doors to anyone and

everyone who would come and join her in a Thanksgiving feast.

"'Twere the old Mrs. Miller's idea durin' the Great Depression, when things were nigh on as bad as they are now in some parts of these here hills," Looty had explained to Ellis weeks before. "'Course, it started out a potluck, with everybody bringin' somethin' ta share. But pretty soon the family just took over, and we been doin' it ever since."

"Must cost a heap of money," Ellis said, thinking aloud, ever appreciative of the way Looty kept track of her nickels.

"That's no lie," the woman said with a snort, puffing her way out of the chair. "But I reckon I ain't got nothin' better to spend it on seein' as I'm alone now. 'Sides," she added, a sad note creeping into her husky voice. "I'd be asittin' here alone all day if I didn't welcome in the hungry and the homeless . . . and anyone else carin' to break bread with me."

With a certain regret Ellis declined supper with the LaSalles and volunteered to help Looty that day. Not for money, but because of the unique new feelings she was carrying inside her.

For the first time in her life the world seemed right. It was good and on her side. Not since Effie Watson had passed away had she had friends and loved ones to share the holidays with. Best of all, she had over a thousand dollars saved up and packed into the seat of the old pickup truck. One final blessing would have made her life perfect. . . .

The weather faired off by midday, and the unmistakable scent of Thanksgiving filled the diner. Looty, Ellis, and several other generous women had been cooking and freezing their labors for weeks. Everything was made from scratch, from family recipes that had been handed down from daughter to daughter for generations. In fact, a near riot had erupted when Anne LaSalle, having lunch at the diner a few days earlier, had suggested in her very northern and highly practical fashion the convenience of store-bought pumpkin pies!

Friends, neighbors, and an occasional stranger came from far and wide to spend a traditional Thanksgiving with Looty. Most were elderly, most were alone, most were down on their luck, and most had nowhere else to go. But there were also those who came and brought contributions, either in currency or consumables.

When the counter space and tables were filled, folks began to line the walls, plates in hand, eating while they waited for a place to sit. Ellis couldn't remember seeing so many people in one place before. The first two hours were a steady stream of hungry people who were grateful for a warm meal and people to share it with.

Ellis served mashed potatoes, sweet potatoes, and a variety of vegetable dishes until she thought her hands would drop off at the wrists. She smiled at everyone and swapped howdies with those she knew. She felt more a part of the town than she ever had in Stony Hollow.

Hardly a dent had been made in the supply of food and drink Looty had arranged for when Ellis began to recognize individuals coming back for a second meal later in the day. Mere weeks had passed since her own stomach had growled with hunger, and her mind fretted at the too-real prospect of starving to death in the cold. She heaped their plates high and hoped the food would sustain them until they could find their next meal.

"You been savin' those yams for me?" Ellis looked up at the sound of Buck LaSalle's voice. He was grinning at her surprised expression. He glanced at Anne, who stood beside him, glowing in her fruitfulness, and added, "Didn't I tell ya it always pays to know someone on the inside?"

"You did," she agreed, winking at Ellis. "And it looks like they cooked enough yams for you to eat your fill and choke a horse with the leftovers."

"I'm savin' space for a couple a Looty's scratch biscuits down yonder there," Bryce said, pointing to his favorite, fixing Looty with a flirty smirk.

"Ah now, don't ya be tryin' to sugar-talk me no more, ya handsome young buck, you," Looty admonished him, feigning insult even as she smoothed the bodice of her dress down over ample curves in a flattered fluster. "I got women in three counties mad as settin' hens 'cuz of the ruckus you been makin' over my biscuits."

"Best biscuits I ever had," he said innocently.

"Well, stop tellin' the husbands," she said, grinning. "I ain't lookin' to get what's left of my hair yanked out over a batch a biscuits."

"Jealous, plain and simple," he said. "That's what it is. And don't think I don't know when I'm gettin' my chain pulled, Looty Miller. Nothin' would please ya more than to have a good knock-down over a platter of your biscuits."

"Fair 'n' true." She cackled heartily. "Fair 'n' true. Now you eat all ya can hold there, boy, and come back for more, ya hear? God bless ya for comin'.'"

"He done a good thing, settin' ya down here, Looty." And in a slightly louder voice, he said, "Now if He could just get my brother to move on down the line, away from the yams, we'd all have somethin' to be truly thankful for."

Buck muttered something under his breath, and Bryce's green eyes twinkled, teasing and warm, taking on a familiar passion when he turned them on Ellis.

"Hey, beautiful," he said in a voice meant only for the two of them. He held his plate out to her. "What can ya give me here that's sweeter than you?"

"What're y'all doin' here?" she asked, her cheeks burning under Bryce's rather obvious stare. "You were fixin' ta have a big fancy supper at home."

"Without you?" Anne asked, looking as if she'd never consider the idea. "Thanksgiving is a time to be with family, and since you were here, we decided to come here too. Can you sit with us for a while?"

Speechless, moved so deeply it pained her, Ellis stood motionless—serving spoons hanging limply from her hands.

"Sure she can," Looty said, prying the spoons from her fingers and nudging her out of the serving line. "She ain't took her feet off the floor once today. Time she did."

By the time she'd gathered her plate of food and joined the LaSalles in a window booth, she was thinking a bit more clearly and feeling the full significance of their actions.

"I . . . I'd like to put up the blessin'," she said timidly, knowing it was Buck's privilege as the eldest male at the table. "If ya wouldn't mind."

"We'd be honored, Ellis," Buck said.

She took Bryce's hand in hers and he took up Anne's, who in turn took Buck's, who reached across the table to spread his big hand over her fingers, and they solemnly bowed their heads.

"Dear Lord," she started in a soft voice. "This here's Ellis callin' on Ya, and I'm askin' Ya to forgive me for the harsh words I used against Ya last time we spoke. I didn't know what Ya had in mind for me, and I didn't trust Ya like I should of. . . . I'm sorry, 'cuz I can see now that You was plannin' on me comin' to Webster all along and fallin' in with this here family of good, kind people. I sure don't deserve Your carin' for me and watchin' out for me all these years—and I keep wonderin' what it was I did when I was young that makes Ya love me so, but whatever Your reasons, I'm mighty grateful. I'll be goin' back to Stony Hollow come early spring, and I know You'll be travelin' with me, keepin' me strong, and I thank Ya ahead for that." She glanced up at the LaSalles and continued, "We're one and all grateful for our good health, for steady work, and for having people to share this day with. We're greatly pleased to be lookin' forward to the birth of Buck and Anne's baby, and ask Ya to watch over mother and child durin' the birthin'." She paused and looked up again, worried. "Am I forgettin' anything?"

"Thank you for Ellis," they said without lifting their

heads or making eye contact or even a partial smirk among them. "Amen."

Christmas was a blessed holiday. Truly. Not merely in the eyes of every person who celebrated it in the world, but in Ellis's eyes as well.

She hadn't received a Christmas gift since she was ten years old. Effie had sewn her a new dress that year—a blue dress, the color of her eyes, with lace around the collar, she recalled as she tied a paper ribbon about the last of the gifts she'd made for Bryce, Buck and Anne, Looty, Tug Hogan, too, if she could work up the nerve to give it to him.

She smiled thinking of Bryce's complaints of eating more rabbit stew in the last month than he'd eaten in his entire lifetime and grinned as she conjured up his expression when he would realize why on Christmas morning.

"Ya reckon ya got 'em all yet?" he'd asked, leaning back after two bowls of her stew, rubbing his stomach contentedly.

"All what?" she'd asked.

"All them poor little bunnies ya been trapping these past weeks? We got minks and foxes out there too. Opossums and muskrats."

"You complainin' about your supper?" she asked, a warning light that she had learned from Anne blinking in her eyes.

He grinned. "No ma'am. I know better. Just bein' concerned about my environment is all. Thought I'd ask if you'd like to try ice fishin' in the mornin'."

They'd eaten rabbit stew twice again after that in order for her to get enough pelts for the fur-lined slippers she'd poured so much love into making.

"Ellis? It's Anne," she heard after a soft tap on the door. "May I come in, please?"

"'Course," she said, bouncing off the bed to open the door. Anne, looking more like a beach ball than a

pregnant woman, rolled into the room with a large box
wrapped in shiny pink paper, an enormous white bow
nestled on the top. "So ya bought Buck the new Sunday
suit after all," Ellis said, chuckling, liking the way the
husband and wife were trying to outgive and outsmart
each other. Buck had been by earlier and asked her to
hide a music box he'd found at the last minute for
Anne. That brought the gift count hidden under her bed
to four for Anne and three for Buck. . . .Well, four for
Buck now. "Did ya decide on the black or the dark
blue?"

"Well, actually, I went back and bought him flannel
shirts," Anne said, smiling and shrugging hopelessly.
"He likes them better, and a second suit would wear out
on the hanger anyway."

Ellis took the box and got down on her knees to place
it under the bed with the others, saying, "Maybe it's
just as well. If the box is this big for flannel shirts, the
box for a whole suit wouldn't fit under here."

"No, Ellis." Anne put a halting hand on her shoulder.
"That one's for you."

"Me?" She pulled the other half of the box back out
from the hiding place and laid it on the floor in front of
her, pulling her hands away to hold them nervously in
her lap.

"Open it, Ellis. Buck and I decided you'd get more use
out of it if we gave it to you a little early, before the party
tonight."

The box with its shiny paper and big fluffy bow were
gift enough. It was too grand to open.

"Please. Open it, Ellis." Anne came to the floor beside
her with no little effort, and as if somehow knowing that
the beauty of the box had Ellis spellbound, she slipped
the top off with paper and bow intact. "Go ahead, Ellis."

She pulled back the layers of tissue paper as if she
were expecting to find religious relics or something so
fine and fragile, it would shatter at the touch of light.

Ten years was a long time, but the thrill of pulling a
bright blue dress from a gift box was no less poignant.

Her throat felt thick and tight and tears gathered in the corners of her eyes. Where the ten-year-old Ellis had held up a homemade dress styled and fit for a ten-year-old, a twenty-year-old Ellis pressed a store-brought dress styled simply with buttons down the front and lace around the collar to her adult body. And where the child Ellis had pranced around the house for Effie and the boys to see, the woman Ellis dressed slowly, putting on the slip and pantyhose she'd found in the bottom of box with the low-heel white shoes that matched the lace trim on the dress, and descended the stairs slowly, wanting only one special someone to see her.

Bryce was standing in the living room, off to one side, legs braced, feeling anxious, trying to hold a coherent conversation with his buddy, Jim Doles.

It was the second Christmas party they'd had since Anne had settled into their lives, and he'd enjoyed the last one tremendously. The house was decorated and crowded with their favorite people, food and drink abounded, but still he was pensive. It was Ellis's first party. She wasn't expected to serve the guests or walk in the background making sure everything went smoothly. She was to be a guest, honored and welcome.

"What if I can't think of anything to say, or if I spill somethin'? Or what if I spill somethin' *on* somebody?" She'd groaned in the darkness. "What if someone laughs at me, and I get mad and—"

"Shh," he'd hushed her, rolling over in the bed to lock her securely in his arms. "Nothin' is gonna go wrong, I promise." He planted a kiss on her temple. "You know most everybody who's comin', and anyone who's met ya loves ya. I've never seen a girl twist so many people 'round her little finger in so short a time."

"It's 'cuz of you that they . . ."

"No." He was adamant. "It's you they care about, Ellis. Folks might tolerate ya 'cuz you're someone I care about, but they go the extra distance to be your friend 'cuz they like *you.*"

"Ya think so?"

He lifted his head and kissed her soundly, with confidence and surety. "I know so." His mouth covered hers once more as he rolled his body atop hers. Fingers that fidgeted anxiously at her chest were disentangled, separated, and drawn up above her head. "The easiest thing I ever did . . . the best thing I ever did, was fall in love with you." He nuzzled her neck, forged a path of delight along the valley between her breasts, drove her wild as he took her left nipple gently between his teeth. She freed her hands to hold him close, arching her back, releasing her thoughts and worries. "The hard part is lettin' go of ya when we're done makin' love and lettin' ya out of my sight when we leave for work in the mornin'." His kisses were increasingly aggressive and possessive; his hands were demanding, and she wallowed in the sensations of being loved and wanted. "It's hard for me not to be jealous of the time ya spend with other people, and it's hard for me to know that I can't give ya the moon and stars, like ya deserve." She pulled his face toward hers and wrapped her legs around his waist. He was the moon and the stars, more than she'd ever dreamed of having. And she needed him.

He returned her kiss but pulled away, smoothing her hair back from her face, needing to speak the words in his heart. "It's hard not to be proud of ya, Ellis. Hard not to admire your strength. Hard knowin' ya don't need me to have what ya want out of life. . . . But lovin' ya is easy. Easy for me and easy for everybody else."

"Show me, then," she'd whispered. "Now. Love me now, Bryce, and don't ever stop."

He sighed, and a familiar longing clutched low in his abdomen. His gaze wandered restlessly over the Christmas merrymakers as he debated going up to her room and coaxing her down to the party . . . or maybe throwing a private party of their own.

His eyes gravitated toward the staircase when a low murmuring rippled through the room.

Ellis. Somehow he was at the bottom of the stairs watching her take each step, timid and self-conscious, when she should have swooped into the crowd like a queen among commoners. An angel among sinners.

Her golden crown of hair haloed her face, pulled up at the sides and secured with a white ribbon, cascading down to the middle of her back. And the dress . . . Well, he hadn't seen her in a dress before. It was . . . inspiring. He wanted to remove it. Slowly. Explore the very female, very womanly aspects it suggested. And legs! Well, he'd seen her legs before, but somehow, sheathed in nylon, her feet in feminine shoes instead of boots . . . well, hell! The whole picture she presented was pure erotica for him.

She came face to face with him on the second to last step, and she was frowning.

"Well?" she asked, her uneasiness making her sound irritated. "Why are ya lookin' at me like that? Don't I look fine? The dress is so beautiful. . . . But on me, maybe . . ."

"The dress is fine. You're beautiful," he said, dazed, struggling to appear somewhere near normal in his behavior. He stepped back and pretended to reexamine the dress, frowning. "But something's missin'."

"Ya dolt! Are ya crazy? She's as pretty as a picture," those who gathered behind him muttered, glaring at him.

"Ya lost your mind, boy?" Looty Miller inquired sternly, elbowing her way to the front of the crowd. "I ain't seen a prettier gal in a year of Sundays. Ellis, pay him no mind, ya hear? Ya look good enough to eat."

"I'd march her all the way down to the front pew," Wilbur Jordan said.

"So would I," Bryce said, glowering at the old man who was still boasting that he'd taught Ellis to two-step. He looked back at her, saw the uncertainty in her eyes, and smiled, saying, "But I still think there's somethin' missin'. Somethin' that would make this . . . this vision perfect."

He snapped his fingers as if hitting on the answer, and taking Ellis by the hand, led her across the room to the Christmas tree. Like magic, he reached into the thick, heavily decorated boughs of the tree and pulled out a small box.

"This is for you," he said, placing it in the palm of her hand.

Lordy. Another gift. From Bryce. She swallowed the tears at the back of her throat. Her hands were shaking. "Shouldn't . . . shouldn't I wait till mornin'? I've already opened . . ."

He leaned forward to murmur in her ear. "There's another for the mornin'. Open this one now. It's all right. It's allowed."

She looked up to see him smile his encouragement; tenderness and affection glowing in his eyes. She smiled back and turned her attention to the little package in her hand.

"Ah," she gasped. "What a pretty little box!"

"Open it!" several women, including Anne and Looty, called out at once, grinning at one another, all of whom had seen similar boxes before.

Inside, hanging on a sparkling box-link chain of gold was a small pendant with a heart-shaped cluster of diamonds dangling at its center.

Thoroughly dazzled, she stared at the necklace until her eyes burned, and for several long moments, she allowed herself to forget who she was, where she came from, and how she had come to be.

She was shaking her head and searching for the right words to refuse his gift when Bryce bent to her ear once more and whispered, "Wear it for tonight. I wanna see how you look in it. We can fight about it later if you're still of a mind too."

Their gazes met, hers very serious, his curiously triumphant. She took the necklace from the box and lifted her hair high and away from her neck. He fastened his heart-shaped pendant around her neck.

It was New Year's Eve before she realized that she could no more remove it than she could cut out her own heart.

"Ya look beautiful in this little necklace," he said, grinning mischievously, toying with it, his fingers brushing sensuously against her skin.

Ellis experienced a full-scale body blush and brushed his hand away.

"I wish ya wouldn't talk like that here," she told him, glancing around the crowded Steel Wheel, her senses in turmoil, her lips barely suppressing a smile. "What if somebody hears ya?"

"Then they'll agree with me. They'll butt right in and say, 'You're right, Bryce, she does look beautiful in that necklace.'"

"Ah, you." She slapped at him playfully and covered the heat in her cheeks with her hands. "Shame on ya for doin' this to me."

He threw his head back and laughed heartily before he covered her hands with his and kissed her smack on the mouth.

It was a typical scene of their life of late. Happy. Loving. Playful. Since the wee hours of Christmas morning it had been a favorite game of theirs to make references to the necklace and the way she looked in it . . . wearing nothing else. Bryce would always say she looked beautiful, but she was less sure and often needed to undress for another opinion.

Loving and making love filled the vast voids in her soul, in the spirit that for so long had been beaten down and trudged upon. This was especially true after Bryce explained the precautions he was taking not to give her a baby before she wanted one. It endeared him to her all the more for his selflessness, and it freed many of the fears and inhibitions she had regarding the act of loving. Liberated from any unwanted consequences, she acquired a healthy interest in and appetite for sex, which Bryce was all too happy to satisfy for her.

And they loved. Sometimes it was slow, steamy, and solemn. Sometimes it was fast, fevered, and fun. Most often it was a combination of both. And always, always, she was content.

Well . . . almost content. As soon as she could get back to Stony Hollow . . . As soon as she could find the right moment to tell Bryce . . . Then she would be content. Soon. Soon.

"Anne and Buck are here," she heard Bryce say, his words fracturing her troubled thoughts. "Come sit with us for a while."

"And lose my job?"

"Then try to be somewhere close at midnight. I'll find ya."

They noticed the light-footed Wilbur Jordan motioning her over to the table where he sat with his wife. She slid off her stool and turned back to him, grinning and teasing him with her eyes. "Well, if you don't find me, Wilbur will."

She left him sputtering as she sashayed over to the Jordans' table.

"Look at the two of ya, all decked out and ready to howl," she said, greeting them warmly, wondering if she and Bryce would be as obviously in love as the Jordans in fifty years. "Ya look real pretty tonight, Miss Bernice."

"Thank you, dear," the old woman replied. "But I'm afraid I've seen a few too many New Years to be pretty anymore."

"Horse pucky!" Wilbur exclaimed. "Bernie, you're as pretty tonight as the night I met ya, told ya so before we left the house tonight."

Bernice giggled, and if the lighting had been better, Ellis might have seen her blushing.

"What can I get ya to drink?" she asked, smiling fondly.

"Hillbilly!" came a familiar roar from the back of the bar.

Ellis ignored it, though it vibrated every vertebra in her back with malice. To spare her the ordeal, the other barmaids had taken to waiting on Reuben Evans whenever possible. She kept her attention focused on the Jordans.

"Bernice wants one of them wine and soda pop flip things she likes to drink, and I'll take my usual," Wilbur said, his facial features tensing when Reuben Evans called out again.

"Anythin' to eat?"

"Not just yet, maybe later," he said, and motioning with his head he added, "You watch your step around that one, hear?"

She nodded and went to two more tables nearby before returning to the bar. The Steel Wheel was hopping and everyone was busy. Evans called out twice more before she arrived at his table.

"What can I get ya to drink?" she asked, using the exact words she used on all the customers, but not necessarily the same tone of voice.

"Ya took your damned sweet time gettin' here," Evans groused. From the smell of him she guessed that he'd started his celebrating early—maybe the day before. He was rumpled and glassy eyed as well, three sure signs of drunkenness that put her senses on red alert.

"I had other orders to take and I'm here now, so what'll ya have?" She noticed he was sitting alone and felt a slight twinge of pity for the man. His nasty disposition had slowly driven away any friends he'd had. The New Year would find him alone and lonely, and she was sorry for that. It was a state she knew well and wouldn't wish on the lowest vermin.

"I don't like the way you're talkin' to me, hillbilly."

"I'm sorry," she said, aware of Bryce's presence in the bar and what he'd do if Evans got out of hand with her. It was best to swallow a little pride and try to keep him calm. "If y'all just tell me what it is you're wantin', I'll be happy to fetch it for ya."

"I'm wantin' you," he said, moving like a lightning bolt to grasp her arm. He pulled her toward him. His breath soured her stomach. "But you're thinkin' you're too high and mighty for me 'cuz ya been sleepin' with LaSalle." The fat was in the fire now, she knew, her skin crawling under his touch. The insults were nothing new, but this was the first time he'd touched her physically. "But ya ain't nothin' special, ya bitch. You're just like all the others, even my Liddy. I'll show ya what a real man can do, make ya feel like ya never felt before, make ya do things ya never thought ya would. You'll be comin' back beggin' for—"

"Get your filthy hands off her."

Both Ellis and Evans turned their heads to see Bryce, a tower of rage, looming above them. She'd been expecting him, but still he surprised her.

"You deaf?" he asked when they remained motionless, one amazed by the transformation of the man she loved into a vicious looking animal, the other well pleased with the result of his endeavors.

"Nah. I ain't deaf," Evans said, slurring his words even as his eyes glinted with a purpose. "Just surprised ya ain't willin' to share what's yours when ya was so free 'n' easy 'bout sharin' what was mine."

Ellis was incredulous. Not by the man's words, but by the fact that he would speak at all in the face of the danger Bryce presented. She remained stonelike, bent over the table, watching the venom gathering in Evans's eyes as he prepared to strike, waiting for her opportunity to break away.

"Ya don't want her, Reuben, ya want me. Let her go."

"Well now, I don't know. But you bein' the authority and all, maybe ya'd tell me if these here hillbillies are as poor in bed as they are at everthin' else they do?"

"Let her go, ya son of a bitch," Bryce said through clenched teeth. "If we have to come to blows, we'll take it outside."

"Afraid she'll see what a feather-legged coward ya are? Ya got your pals out there awaitin' on me? Afraid she'll see the way ya gotta sneak around to get what ya want? The way ya sneaked around with Liddy?"

"Liddy and I didn't have to sneak around. We stepped out in front of the whole town. Everyone knew ya deserted her and ran out on your kids like the no 'count lowlife ya are."

Reuben's eyes shifted first to the left and then the right, looking into the faces of the people surrounding them. People who knew who he was and what he'd done. People who valued home and family second only to God. People who believed in just deserts and had been watching this hash simmering for months.

"Let her go now, Reuben, or I'll knock ya four ways from Sunday." The threat was made simply.

But Reuben was a man who had a tendency to overwind his watches, and he was dumber than a barrel of hair. Like a shot-putter, he propelled Ellis away from him, backward into Bryce's arms, using his other hand to draw a long-blade knife from his boot, brandishing it in the air between him and the young lovers.

A split second later he was face down on the floor and disarmed after Peter Harper, Jim Doles, Buck, and Tug Hogan appeared out of nowhere and jumped him from behind. The fight was over before it began.

"If ya wanna stir up a dust with your fists, that's one thing," Tug's voice boomed out over the anxious crowd. "But I won't abide no knife-flashin' in my bar. Ya get your sorry ass up off my floor, Reuben Evans, and don't ya come back till ya can hold your corners up square."

Either too stunned or too drunk to lift his head off the floor, Reuben had to be dragged to the door by his four attackers while the crowd rumbled, reenacting or predicting the probable victor of the fracas that never occurred.

"You okay? Did he hurt ya?" Bryce asked, turning her to face him so he could see for himself.

"No," she said, watching the metal doors close after Evans. She looked at Bryce then, glad to see that his temper had gone as quickly as it had arrived. "I'm fine. But it ain't over, is it, Bryce? I . . . he'll be back, won't he?"

He shook his head once. "He's after me, but the whole town's against him 'cuz of Liddy. . . . 'Cuz of you too. He ain't a stupid man, Ellis, he's just mad as hell. My guess is that he'll crawl off in a couple a days, and we won't hear of him again." Seeing the doubt in her eyes, he grinned. "He sure ain't comin' back tonight, and we're gonna be startin' a whole new year together in less than an hour. What'd ya do with all your smiles? Stick 'em in your pocket?"

She slipped him a small one. "That's better." He bussed her lips. "I'll get Buck to take my truck home. That way I can go back with you and you can show how pretty ya look in the necklace again." He smirked and wagged his brows comically. The least she could do in return for his efforts was to laugh at him.

Tug Hogan had hired a live band for the night, local boys who played western and bluegrass on occasion, but who also had families they supported working at the textile mill like most everybody else in Webster.

Father Time marched out at midnight, and Baby New Year was herald in with cheers, noise makers, and a lively round of "Auld Lang Syne." Everybody danced. Everyone.

"I gotta stop," Ellis cried, falling into a chair breathless, wobble kneed, and ecstatically happy. "I gotta stop or I'll die."

Bryce sat across from her taking a long sip of his beer to quench his thirst. Buck and Anne had left shortly after twelve. Their empty glasses were still on the table.

"Where in tarnation is the barmaid when ya need her," she asked, watching the last drop of fluid disappear when he licked it from his lips.

"Ah." He looked shamefaced. "I'm sorry. I forgot ya didn't have one. I'll be back in a sec."

"No. It was a joke. I can fetch one—I think I should go back to work anyway," she said, looking around uneasily. One dance had turned into several in all the frivolity. She wasn't sure how much time had elapsed, but she was sure it was considerable.

"Nah. Everybody parties after midnight, and folks serve themselves. It's tradition here. Look there at Tug dancin' with Mary Jo."

It was a sight to see.

She grew lax, listening to the music and watching the people dance, waiting for Bryce to return. With time to notice such things, she began to suspect there was something wrong with the drums . . . or maybe the drummer had tipped too many. There was an odd, irregular downbeat, over and over that didn't hold with the rhythm of the music. She turned her head when she heard Bryce call a farewell to a friend, then turned back to the band.

"Here ya go," he said seconds later, setting a soft drink in front of her. He'd debated over getting her something stronger to toast the new year with, but knowing her aversion to spirits, chose her usual libation instead.

"Thank ya," she said, picking it up and taking long refreshing gulps.

"The drummer's drunk," Bryce said in passing, making no judgment. "Have ya noticed the way he keeps addin' extra beats?"

"I did." She grinned and leaned back in her chair with a hand to her heart. "I thought it was me in the beginnin'. My heart was beatin' so fast, I thought everybody could hear it."

His head tilted to one side as he watched her, her face radiant with happiness.

"Ya sure are pretty, Ellis," he said, not really meaning to compliment her, merely stating a fact.

She sat forward again, slipping her fingers between his hands. "Ya keep tellin' me that. But the only time I feel pretty is when ya look at me the way ya do."

His face came closer, and she knew he was going to kiss her. She wanted him to. She was eager.

"Bryce! Get out here quick!" came a male voice from the main door. It was the man he'd waved good-bye to moments before. Bryce was at the door before Ellis could push her chair away from the table. The man was still shouting. "He's really lost it this time. Look at him."

Bryce stopped cold in the doorway, shocked and bewildered, unable to believe what he was seeing. By the time Ellis got there, they were three or four bodies apart, and she couldn't see a thing.

"For crissake," she heard him mutter before he uncorked the exit and let the people pour out into the cold, snowy parking lot.

It was Ellis's turn to stand in disbelief and horror and watch as a big blue truck ran full throttle into the back of her old, already battered pickup. Before her eyes the driver backed up at a right angle, shifted gears, and plowed into the right tail end.

"No," she heard herself say in a weak, feeble voice. "No. Stop that."

It was then that she noticed Bryce running alongside the truck, making one attempt after another to grab the door handle without getting run over in the process. He shouted at the driver, and her gaze lifted. Reuben Evans sat behind the steering wheel, a crazed, vengeful, and absolutely determined expression etched deeply in his features.

She willed her feet to move her forward, thinking that there was something she could do to help Bryce. The rear end of her pickup looked like an accordion, and when the sound of the impact and whine of bending metal came to her a third time, she knew she'd misjudged the drummer. He hadn't been silly on spirits and out of sync. The irregular beats had been Evans's very deliberate and very rhythmic destruction of her vehicle.

"Stop," she shouted, her shock fading to outrage.

"Somebody call the law. That's my pickup. Why is he doin' that?"

She'd marched out to the middle of the parking lot shouting and waving her arms when a set of mindful hands restrained her, pulled at her, and staggered her backward toward safety.

"No. He's gotta be stopped," she cried to her unseen and uncared about caretaker. "That's all I got. It's . . ." She froze. A whisper escaped on a breath of terror. "The money."

With a sudden jerk she broke loose of her protective restraints and bolted for the old pickup. She hadn't gone ten feet before she was captured again. She heard a familiar male voice trying to calm her, reason with her, but her strongest instincts had already taken over.

She fought like a bobcat to free herself, cringing from the inside out when the slam of metal on metal penetrated her consciousness.

"Please. Let go," she screamed, digging her nails into flesh, thrashing her legs about in search of any obstacle in her path. "The money. Please. I . . . Let go of me!"

Somewhere in the back of her mind she was still keeping track of Bryce and his efforts to stop the madman. She registered that he'd reached the handle, that he'd been dragged several feet before he'd pushed himself away from the truck, and that he cursed proficiently and profusely before announcing that the doors were locked.

"Get your shotgun, Tug," she heard him bellow into the crowd of people behind her, her arms flailing in her attempts to pull at her captor's hair. "We'll blow out his tires."

A microsecond later the big blue truck rammed the dilapidated old pickup once more. Sparks shot from the pickup's bowels before tongues of fire lapped across its belly, licking out at both sides.

Ellis's scream split the night wide open. An animal instinct deep inside her snapped and spilled superhuman juices into her bloodstream. With another cry that went beyond anything earthly, she tore loose of the hands that were keeping her from the most important thing in her life.

She ran in front of the truck, oblivious to the fact that she'd come within mere feet of being crushed under its wheels as it sped out of the parking lot into the cover of darkness.

Nor was she particularly alert to the steady flame burning its way into the gas tank when she tried to yank open the door on the driver's side of the pickup.

The door was stuck. She beat on the window with no effect and went back to bashing and banging on the door to get it to open.

"Ellis!" It was Bryce. "For crissake, have ya lost your mind? This thing's gonna blow up any minute." He took her hand and attempted to pull her away, but she wasn't leaving without her money. "Ellis! It's too late. You can't save it."

"I got to. Bryce, help me! My money."

He took both her hands this time, and when pulling and dragging her wasn't fast enough, he bent low and threw her over his shoulder like a sack of potatoes.

"Get your damned hands offa me," she screamed, pummeling his back with her fists. "Put me down. Bryce! Stop. Please. Help me. My money. I have to have my money. It's in the seat. Bryce! Listen to me. It's in the seat. The seat, Bryce. I have to have that money."

"It ain't worth it," he said, panting, weak with fear and effort as he set her on the ground on the far side of the building. Others had taken shelter there as well, but just to make sure that everyone was safely concealed, he turned and poked his head around the corner.

His mind tripped beyond shock when Ellis shot past like a dart. The truck was her bull's-eye.

"Dammit to hell," he said, taking a flying leap, tackling her facedown in the snow an instant before the truck blew up.

The noise was deafening. An invisible force stomped across their prone bodies so quickly and so stunningly, they weren't sure when it began or when it ended—only that it had happened. And then there was silence but for an occasional piece of metal hitting the ground.

Eleven

As if in slow motion, Bryce lifted his head, and when he saw that it was safe to do so, he rolled his body off hers to lie on his back looking up at the stars. They seemed unreal. Too far away. Too peaceful to be a part of what had just happened. What *had* just happened? The entire episode flashed through his mind and seemed more unreal than the stars.

He could feel Ellis stirring at his side.

"Gawd. I feel like I been shot at twice and missed," he said, a general comment on how lucky he felt to be alive.

He knew he was a bit put out with Ellis and that he had a few pointed remarks he wanted to make to her, but he wasn't sure what they were yet.

He was bounced back to reality with a jolt when her fist met his chest like a jackhammer on concrete. The wind whooshed out of him and refused to come back.

"Why did ya stop me?" she cried, tears streaming down her cheeks, the mist of her angry words rising in the frigid air.

"Why did I . . ." He gasped for air and struggled to raise his head off the ground. She began to rant.

"Ya knew it was important. I worked hard for it. I need it. Why did ya stop me? I hate you." She hit him again. "I hate you, ya hear? Ya shouldn'ta stopped me. I'll never get him back now. It'll take me too long to start over. He'll forget how to talk. Granny Yeager *never* talks. He'll forget me." Her voice quivered heartwrenchingly. "He won't remember who I am or how much I love him. It's been too long. He won't remember me. Ya shouldn'ta stopped me." Sobbing, she crumpled into a heap.

Feeling as if he were living in an extended nightmare, he automatically reached out to comfort her, though he didn't know why. Nothing she'd said made sense to him. Who wouldn't remember her? What other *him* did she love? All he knew for sure was that she was in great pain. He could hear it in her voice, feel it in every fiber of his being.

She pushed his hand away and cried harder. He decided to deal with the only complaint he knew anything about.

"Money ain't worth dyin' for," he said. He touched her again with the same result. His need to ease her pain was a tangible thing, as strong as any other urge he'd known. "Payin' off a debt is a good thing, but no one expects ya to die doin' it."

"I would," she moaned. "I'd have done anything."

"It's only money, Ellis," he said, frustration getting the better of him. She gripped her abdomen and groaned painfully as if someone had stabbed her. His concern and helplessness made him anxious and nervous. He didn't know how to help her, what to say, what to do.

He bent his head until their faces were only a breath apart and whispered reassuringly, "We'll get the money, Ellis. Soon. I promise. We'll figure out somethin' and pay off the debt. We'll work it out together. I promise."

Profound relief washed over him when he felt her arm snake around his neck, pulling him closer.

"I gotta have him with me," she murmured, still

crying, her words barely understandable. "He needs me. I need him."

"Who, Ellis? Who do you need?" His heart stopped until she answered.

"My baby. I need my baby, Bryce."

Mystified and profoundly hurt in a way he couldn't describe, he slowly pulled away from her. For several long seconds he watched as she wept in misery—in an agony greater than any she'd told him about.

"Is she hurt?"

He looked up into Bernice Jordan's kind face and shook his head. She bent to tuck a coat tight about Ellis's shivering body. He shook his head once again to clear away the cobwebs of confusion.

"No. She's . . . upset," he said. He looked around at the familiar faces that had gathered, worried and as dazed as he was. "Could someone . . . give us a lift home?"

He scooped her up out of the snow and carried her all the way home on his lap like a small child. She clung to him weakly, and her crying subsided. An occasional sob racked her body. He murmured soft, unintelligible words in her ear while his mind ticked rapidly, sorting through information, calculating, reasoning.

A door on the second floor closed quietly. Moments later Bryce heard Anne's footfall on the stairs. He waited, his nerves jumping restlessly under the surface of his skin. He hated being helpless, useless. It was the plight of his life. Now more than ever before he wanted to do something. He wanted to make a difference.

"She's sleeping," Anne said at the bottom of the stairs. It was all she said.

He watched Anne lower herself into a chair and was about to blast her with questions when he noticed the trembling of her hands. In a movement that spoke of extreme control, she set her elbow on the arm of the chair and lowered her forehead into it.

"I want to break something," she said, her voice strained with anger. "Somebody's arm or their leg or their face."

Buck, always near her, always close, pulled a footstool to her chair and settled himself on it.

"What happened?" he asked quietly, giving her time to collect her emotions. "Where's her baby?"

"She . . ." Her chin quivered as tears brimmed her eyes. She cleared her throat to dislodge the words. "She had to leave it in Stony Hollow."

"Why?" Why was all Bryce wanted to know. Why? Why? Why? Why did she need the money? Why had she left her baby behind? Why hadn't she told him?

Anne looked at him and shook her head. "She didn't have any other option." She sighed, heavy and deep, her hand lifting to caress her abdomen and the small miracle within. "I can't even imagine having to make the choice she did—but it was the only choice she had."

"Why? How could she leave her child?"

"Don't judge her harshly, Bryce. . . ."

"I'm not judging. I'm trying to understand," he said, running an agitated hand through his hair.

"The baby was . . . unexpected, from what I could gather," she said, speaking quickly to fill Bryce in on the details. "Her husband hadn't wanted it, with grown sons of his own, but . . . there it was. When he died, he left Ellis nothing. But he did include the baby. He left him an equal parcel of land—the same as he left his other sons."

She extended her hand, flexing her fingers as if groping for something solid. Buck covered it securely, with big hands that could handle most anything.

"She loves you very much, Bryce. You're the only man who's ever been kind to her. Did you know that?"

He shook his head and then nodded. He wasn't sure what he knew anymore.

"When her husband died, it was like . . . open season on Ellis. The sons saw her as fair game, and their wives saw her as an unattached female and felt threatened—not unreasonably from what Ellis has told me." She hesitated. "Ellis moved out. She and the baby went back to the old woman, the one who taught her the potions?"

"Yeager."

"That's the one. But the old lady didn't want her back. She made it very clear, but she took them in temporarily until Ellis could find her own place and get settled. She looked for work, but there either wasn't any or no one would hire her. . . . That part was a little garbled. Eventually she hit on the idea of selling the baby's share of the land and using the money to relocate in a city. The brothers"—she might just as well have said the snakes if the intonation of her voice was any indicator—"wouldn't hear of it. They threatened to take her baby."

Both Bryce and Buck could have pointed out that such an act would have been illegal, and even if they'd taken her to court, they still would have had to prove that Ellis was an unfit mother—but neither said a word. Justice in the nooks and crannies of the Appalachian Mountains bore little resemblance to the American legal system—less to its ideal. Change came slowly as the people clung to old ways that had serviced them well enough for over two hundred years. Illegitimate and homeless, Ellis would have had a better chance of putting hell out with a bucket of water than she had fighting the Johnson brothers.

"She'd never worked for wages before . . . only her keep. She knew she had to leave Stony Hollow to make a life for herself and for her baby, but . . ." Anne started to cry outright, silently, as if she were unaware of it. "She said that even if she ate nothing herself, the baby would starve to death faster than she would. She didn't know if she could find work outside Stony Hollow, or a place to live."

She wiped her eyes on the hem of her smock and sniffled loudly. "But she knew the people of Stony Hollow. She knew that the worst that could happen to her baby if she left him there would be that his life would be like hers. They'd work him, shame him, and berate him . . . but they wouldn't let him die."

Tension crackled in the air like firecrackers on the Fourth of July. They tried to imagine the pain and the courage it had taken for Ellis to leave her child and embark into a world she knew nothing about. They couldn't.

"What about the money?" Bryce finally asked. "She said she had a debt to pay."

Anne nodded. "The old woman, that Granny person? Ellis trusts her. She's quiet and to herself, she doesn't speak often, and Ellis was worried that the child would forget how to talk. But apparently the woman is also ornery and unwelcoming, and because of her instincts for healing, the people in Stony Hollow are a little afraid of her. And . . . I guess, in her own peculiar way, she'd been good to Ellis. So she made a deal with the old woman."

"What sorta deal?"

"Well . . ." Anne was thoughtful for a moment, and as an aside, she said, "Actually if this weren't part of a tragic story, it would be funny. But this old woman has outlived her husband and her seven children, and she isn't fond of anyone. . . . And, well, the long and short of it is that Ellis knew she was concerned about being buried properly when, or if, she finally died." She couldn't stop it—and she needed a good laugh anyway. "I'm sorry. This isn't funny." She burst into a fit of laughter.

Bryce and Buck delayed their protests, allowing Anne to laugh until she cried, sensing the hysterical release of emotions she had no other civilized way to let go of.

"I am sorry," she said, wiping her eyes once more and making a supreme effort to control her facial features. "Where was I? Oh yes. Well, Ellis made this deal with the old woman. They gave a letter to the preacher to be opened at the time of the old woman's death, instructing him to contact Ellis—who solemnly vowed to let the preacher know her whereabouts, always, until after the woman died—and then Ellis would come back from wherever she was and see to it the woman was buried properly . . . whatever that means. And in return, the old woman would keep Ellis's child safe from the Johnsons and feed him and be kind to him until Ellis could return for him."

"What was the money for?" Buck asked, snatching the words from his brother's mouth. Bryce was having a hard time keeping up with the story, his mind chewing and digesting each new detail.

"The money was for the old lady's funeral," Anne explained. "So much for the coffin. So much for a new dress out of a catalog. So much for the minister. The woman wanted the entire sum up front in exchange for her promise to Ellis."

"One thousand, five hundred, thirty-six dollars and eighty-seven cents," Bryce uttered the sum absently. In his mind he kept seeing Ellis beating on the door of the ancient pickup, smoke and flames lapping out to get her. "Blown to hell."

"What can we do?" Anne asked both men. "They need to be together, Ellis and her baby."

"Pool our savings? Loan her the money?" Buck suggested.

A derisive snort broke from Bryce. "I'm tapped. Lent most of it to Liddy and spent the rest at Christmas." Nothing to give. Useless again. "She wouldn't take it anyway. We ain't kin and she's got a notion she needs . . . to do . . . everythin' on . . . her own . . ."

His words dwindled and tapered away as the seed of an idea took root in his brain, sprouted, and grew a hundred feet tall. He knew exactly what he could and would do to resolve the situation, could and would do to make Ellis happy, completely happy, and fully content.

A slow grin spread across his lips when his bright gaze caught Anne and Buck staring at him.

"This is gonna work out fine," he said.

"Need help?" Buck asked.

"Like a tomcat needs a weddin' license." Not at all. "I'm goin' up to see her."

"Oh, can't it wait till morning?" Anne protested. "She needs to sleep, Bryce."

"I ain't gonna wake her. I just wanna look at her," he said, grinning like an idiot, extremely pleased with his brainstorm. He stopped midstep. "What's the boy's name?"

"Jonah." Anne twisted in the chair to face him. "She got it from the bible. She said anyone who could be swallowed, carried for three days, and spit up by a big fish would have to be courageous and strong. She said her baby would have to be courageous and strong to grow up in Stony Hollow."

Bryce wasn't smiling when he opened the door to Ellis's room. From across the room he could hear the slow in and out of her breathing. It consoled him. It was a normal sound, a sound of life. The light from the hall cast shadows over her face as he stood looking down at her. But no shadow could hide her beauty.

She was a sweet dreaming baby whose face was like that of an angel. But her real beauty was inside. It couldn't wrinkle with age or be disguised with a mask. She had courage and strength and more heart than was good for her. And she was his.

He crept back to the door, overflowing with the sort of peacefulness one experiences when it occurs to him that just being alive can be so very nice.

He closed the door softly.

But when next he opened it, Ellis was gone.

Twelve

Bryce found his truck parked on the street in front of Looty's diner.

He'd checked the old logging road where he'd first discovered Ellis sleeping in her pickup. Driving to the Steel Wheel, he found it locked up tight on the first day of the New Year. He carefully inspected the hull of the burned-out pickup truck, hoping for some sign that she'd been there before him. Frantic, he stopped anyone he found out and about that morning and asked if they'd seen her.

The sight of his truck bolstered his hopes and sent a tidal wave of relief through his body. But once that was over, he was angry. Angry with himself for acting crazy when he should have known that the *first* thing Ellis would do after a disaster was pull herself up by the bootstraps and go back to work at Looty's. Angry with her for being so . . . Ellis.

He had both angries settled and was just plain glad when he pushed open the diner door.

"Hey, good lookin'," he called his usual greeting to Looty, who immediately wiped her greasy fingers on her apron, then stood arms akimbo, pleased as punch to see him.

"A fine way to start the New Year, I swear," she said,

beaming at him. "The handsomest young buck in eight counties, and me with a batch of biscuits fresh from the oven, no less. Want a couple?"

"Yeah, I would, please." He was feeling a great deal better. Still, to feel perfect, he wanted to see Ellis. "Where's that pretty little gal ya got workin' for ya, Looty? We need to discuss truck stealin' . . . among other things."

"She ain't stole your truck, it's parked there outside," she said, her eyes narrowing as she watched him.

"I was just teasin'. Ya musta heard what happened last night."

"Hmm. A sorry piece a work, that Reuben Evans. Never did cotton to him. Heard they caught him over in Knott County close to dawn sometime."

"Good. I hadn't heard."

"Young Ellis'll be glad to hear he won't be givin' her no more trouble."

A chill shot through his heart. "Ya haven't told her?"

"Didn't know 'bout it when I seen her."

"She ain't here now?"

"Well . . . no. She was here awaitin' on me when I come to open up. Asked for the day off and for the pay I owed her."

"The pay?" he repeated, his mind traveling faster than a greased pig in third gear.

"'Course. After hearin' 'bout what happened, I figured she'd be needin' some. I offered a little extra to tide her over a spell. Said it could be a loan. But she only wanted what was comin' to her."

"And she took the day off?"

"Yep. Said she had somethin' important she had to do today. Said it couldn't wait no longer. She left your truck parked yonder and walked off down the street toward the mo-tel. I been expectin' her back half the mornin' now."

Folks caught the Greyhound Bus in front of McKee's Motel.

"She ain't comin' back, Looty," he said, rising from

the stool beside the counter and heading for the door. "She's gone back to Stony Hollow."

She couldn't stop touching him. For months she'd held a photograph of him in her heart, but seeing him . . . He'd changed. Fractionally taller, a little plumper. He talked faster.

"And see, mama. This is my bunny," Jonah said proudly, his giant blue four-year-old eyes never leaving his mother's face. He watched for her surprise, her pleasure, and her approval of his pet—he watched to make sure she wouldn't disappear again. "Granny said I was a good boy, and if I let her rest in the evenin's and if I took very good care of him, I could keep him. He eats greens. And water. I feed 'im. By myself. He's quiet too. Like me. Not like a dog. He leaves droppin's. That's not so fine."

Ellis nodded, paying grave attention to all the information he had to impart.

"He's a grand bunny, Jonah. How long before he's all mended?" She hadn't forgotten how wonderful it was to watch the animation in his face when he spoke, or his slight lisp, or the way he took deep breaths between gushes of words. She observed his hands, chubby and fumbling one second, agile and precise the next. And his hair—blonde and soft as chick down.

"Granny says maybe next Sunday . . . That's the day she goes to see the preacher. We get to set in Granny's chair while she's away. We don't touch nothin', and we don't go outside. That's 'portant."

She palmed his face, stroking his cheeks with her thumbs while her heart ached. He was too young to be left alone. Too young to be away from his mama. Too young to have to hide.

"You're a fine, *fine* boy, Jonah. I love ya so," she said, struggling to keep her voice from cracking. "Ya know that, don't ya? I love ya more than anythin' else in the whole world. Ya won't forget that, will ya? Ever?"

The light in his eyes flickered out, and he didn't respond.

"Jonah?" She glanced briefly away when the door opened and the widow Yeager stomped the snow off her boots before walking in. "Jonah? Don't ya believe me?"

Light-lashed lids lowered over his eyes, and he bent his face away from her. She gripped the front of her shirt to keep her heart from falling apart.

"Jonah?"

"Ellis?"

"Bryce?" Her hands fell to her son's small shoulders. She stared open-mouthed at the tall male form across the room.

"Visitor," Granny Yeager announced. She wasn't as quick as she once was.

The visitor closed the door and advanced into the two-room dwelling with a deceptively confident step. He stopped several feet away from the mother and child, his eyes riveted on the woman. He studied her long and hard, guessing at her thoughts, questioning her emotions. And when he found no answers, he knew he'd have to resort to words.

"Good bodyguard ya got there," he said, indicating the old widow with his head. Ellis could only nod as she continued to stare. The same question kept spinning around in her head, but it couldn't seem to find an outlet. She saw his gaze lower to Jonah.

"Said he'd walk up the barrel of my shotgun and punch my lights out if I didn't let him see ya," Granny grumbled. She settled herself in a creaky rocking chair. "Pin-headed thing to do, so I figured him harmless."

Adelaide Yeager wasn't accustomed to explaining her actions to anyone, nor did she usually connect more than two words together in a single oration. But nobody seemed impressed. In fact, they may not have heard her at all.

Bryce examined the boy from head to toe. Ellis stood tall and proud, her hands on her son's shoulders. She wanted Bryce's favor, but she was ready to demand his respect.

"You Jonah?" he asked, his soft southern baritone generating nothing but gentleness.

Jonah, who moments earlier had determined that his mama would be going away again—without him—and who had been quietly assessing the stranger who had made his mama go suddenly silent and tense, simply nodded.

"I brought ya somethin'," the man said. "A gift."

He reached into the pocket of his coat and, with a bit of difficulty, pulled out a shiny red toy pickup truck an inch bigger than the palm of his big hand.

Jonah wanted it. Badly. He appealed to a higher authority.

Ellis looked down into her son's face and saw the question . . . and the caution. She smiled. Bryce was one person in the world Jonah could trust.

"Jonah, this here's Mr. LaSalle. He's . . ." How to explain it to a four-year-old? "He's my very best friend. Can ya tell him thank you for the truck?"

He sure could. He even smiled—Ellis's smile—when he went to Bryce, took the truck, and made his loud thank you before falling to an empty space on the floor to test it out.

"What are ya doin' here?" she asked with a half laugh when the question finally took form on her lips. She still couldn't believe he was there.

"I brought somethin' for you too," he said, standing to face her. "A gift."

"Ya came all this way to give me a gift?"

From his other pocket he produced a white envelope and handed it to her. She broke the seal and looked inside, shaking it to count the eighty-seven cents.

"What's this?" she asked, her mouth going dry.

"The money ya need . . . and a little more to get started on," he said, every word leaving a bad taste in his mouth.

There were a variety of questions she could and

wanted to ask but the first one out of her mouth was, "Where'd ya get it from?"

He shrugged. "Ain't important. Thing is, ya got it and now ya can take Jonah outta this place. Start new someplace like ya planned to."

"It is important. Where'd ya get the money? You ain't a rich man."

That hurt. "I told ya it ain't important. What do you know about what I got and what I ain't got?"

"I know ya ain't got any money. Not this kinda money."

"For crissake, Ellis," he shouted, then noticing the frightening effect it had on Jonah, he lowered his voice and said, "Will ya just take it, and get the hell outta here? Ya don't belong here." As it occurred to him, he added, "Ya never belonged here."

"Tell me where ya got it."

"What do you care?" he asked. She was going to pull that independent, "it ain't none of your concern" routine again, and as much as he admired it, it irritated the hell out of him. Especially now, when every breath she took concerned him.

"I care," she said, her tone of voice changing to a tender caress. "I care with all my heart."

That did it! Now he was really confused. Compounded with the intense pain he was feeling, he got angry. But rather than admit it, he attacked.

"Well, ya got a fine way of showin' it," he shouted. Again, he noticed that Jonah didn't appreciate having his mama bellowed at. "Is there a place we can talk? Alone."

Without a word, she walked past him, grabbed her coat from the peg on the wall, went out the door, across the path and the side yard to the wood shed. If he was aiming to give her a thrashing, it was the best place.

She watched as he paced the length of the shed, again and again, choosing his words and battling his temper. When he spoke, she guessed that he'd lost the battle. And she didn't mind a bit.

"Dammit, Ellis! I . . . I . . ." He threw up his hands and growled in utter frustration.

He was, at last, showing her his full ire as she'd expected him to so many times before, without satisfaction. Strange thing, his obvious anger didn't frighten her. Physically or emotionally.

She wasn't the commander of a confederacy of smarts, but she knew when she was in danger, and she knew when she was loved. Bryce loved her; and she trusted him absolutely.

"I'm tryin' to understand why ya didn't tell me about the boy . . . 'cuz of all the things I said about Evans desertin' his and all, and you thinkin' I'd look poorly on you too. But I can't believe you'd just give up and come back here," he said, holding out his hands to show her that he was totally lost to her thinking. "I mean, I . . . Why, Ellis? Ya got folks who love ya and care about ya in Webster. We'da helped ya. And . . . and I know ya don't think ya need a man, but I wouldn't of held ya down. Ya coulda done anythin' with your life. Still can, if ya put the rest of that money to good use and get the hell outta this town." He grasped her forearms and bent his knees to equalize the plain between them. "Take Jonah and go, Ellis. If ya don't wanna live with me, then go somewhere else. But don't let yourself get bogged down in this place because of your pride. You take that money and get as far from here as ya can. That's all I'm asking from ya."

He was the *beatin'est* man! He was finally, truly angry with her, and it was for all the wrong reasons!

"Ain't ya mad that I stole your truck? Or that I set out without tellin' ya?" she asked, scowling at him, wishing that just once he'd react in an appropriate fashion.

"Ya didn't steal my truck, ya left it at Looty's," he said, thrown off track. "And I ain't mad that ya left without tellin' me . . . just . . . just hurt is all."

His hands fell to his sides when he walked away from her.

"Ya thought I was runnin' away from ya. And that I

wasn't comin' back. Ya thought 'cuz I lost all my money last night that I'd give up on my dreams. Well, you ain't gonna get bowlegged totin' *your* brains around, Bryce LaSalle."

He turned to look at her. She was as angry as a rooster in an empty henhouse.

"If brains was dynamite, ya wouldn't have enough to blow your nose. Tomorrow's a whole new day that ain't been touched yet," she told him with a wave of her arm. "I ain't about to waste it here, and I'm . . . I'm . . . insulted that you'd think it of me. I'm insulted that ya don't know how much I love ya. And you're wrong about me not needin' ya in my life. I need ya to love me and to make me feel safe and to make me laugh and . . ." She was losing steam fast. Her voice lowered. "I wouldn't . . . couldn't ever leave ya, Bryce. But I was missin' my baby somethin' fierce."

What air she had left in her lungs was abruptly squeezed out when Bryce scooped her into his embrace, lifting her off the ground to twirl her about.

"Gawd, ya had me scared to death," he said, skimming his mouth over hers, in a hurry to kiss as much of her beautiful face as he could. "Next time leave me a note or somethin', will ya?"

"I bought a two way ticket. I'd have been home by suppertime."

His kiss was hard and deep and greedy. "Just come home."

Rifle fire split the silence of the woods, echoing through the hollow and in their ears.

Granny Yeager stood at the corner of the cabin with her smoking shotgun in hand.

"Nuffa that," she said. "More visitors."

"Jonah," Ellis muttered under her breath, dashing off.

Bryce followed, but at a leisurely pace. He wanted to whistle in the wind, hang upside down in a tree and act like a nut. He was a lucky man, and he knew it.

She was back at the door of the cabin with Jonah in

her arms. She was trying hard not to look too frightened or panicky, but she wasn't succeeding. She knew she still had a few minutes—Granny could smell trespassers a mile off, and she'd warned them off with her shot. Ellis wanted to run into the woods and hide, but thought she ought to stay and explain the situation to Bryce. He was leaning casually against the side of the cabin, happy and content as a goat in a can factory.

"It's the boys. The Johnson brothers," she hissed, whispering as if they might hear her. "I came in through the woods but somebody mighta seen me, and if ya drove through the hollow comin' after me, they'll have heard. They're comin' after Jonah."

"Pay your debt to the old woman, Ellis," he said, unmoved. "I'm of a mind to take ya home and get you and Jonah settled in my house once and for all. Then I'm gonna let ya show me how pretty ya look in that necklace of yours."

"Bryce . . ." He pushed himself away from the wall, looking down the slope of the mountain at two men walking briskly toward them.

"Pay her and we'll go." He started walking out to meet them.

"Bryce . . ." He paid her no heed.

She hesitated on the threshold, torn between keeping her baby safe and trusting Bryce. Not an easy decision for a person who believed that safety and distrust equaled survival.

But mere survival wasn't good enough for her anymore. Jonah's birth had determined that for her. She wanted a life of her own and to pass that freedom on to her son. Stony Hollow destroyed her belief in fairy tales. She wasn't looking for perfect. But she believed in her power to create change. She believed in the plans she'd made for her future. She believed in her dreams. And . . . she believed in Bryce.

Hurriedly, she paid Granny Yeager exactly what she owed and repeated her vow to come back to Stony Hollow to fulfill the rest of the debt. Impulsively, she kissed the old woman's cheek and ran back to the door.

"My bunny," Jonah cried. Ellis looked to the widow, who was touching her cheek as if she could still feel Ellis's kiss.

"Take it," she said gruffly, adding, "Godspeed."

With Jonah on one arm and the rabbit on the other, she stepped from the cabin in time to hear Bryce say, "You wouldn't know a good woman if she walked up and bit ya on the butt. As to her takin' care of the boy, that ain't none of your concern. She and the boy are my family now."

This was all very nice for Ellis to hear. But she did wonder if Bryce had noticed that the brothers were wearing expressions as dark as a pile of black cats, and they were both carrying rifles.

"The hell ya say," the taller of the two brothers said. "She didn't ask to marry again."

"She doesn't have to. Nobody owns her," he said. "That reminds me. I heard she had a problem tryin' to sell the boy's land. If she's still of a mind to, she will."

"Who the hell do ya think you're talkin' to here?" the second, fiercer-looking brother asked. "We been livin' in this here holler all our life. It can be a real treacherous place sometimes. Folks come up here alone and ain't never seen nor heard from again. If you're catchin' my drift."

"I'm catching it. But if you two don't turn them gawd-awful, ugly faces of yours downhill and move them sorry backsides out of my sight in the next second or so, I'm gonna fill 'em full of lead . . . if you're gettin' my drift." He stood there, unarmed, and dared them to call his bluff.

So they did.

Each brother lowered his firearm to Bryce's midsection and turned smiling faces to each other.

"Bryce! No!" Ellis shouted, running mindlessly toward him, skidding to a stop when she felt Jonah clinging to her neck.

Then, like in one of the fairy tales she didn't believe

in, the woods came to life. Chills and a trillion little goose bumps skipped over her body. From out of the snow-laden bushes and behind the trees came twenty or more of Webster's finest citizens. Among them were Tug Hogan, Wilbur Jordan, Jim Doles, Buck LaSalle, Looty Miller, and Pete Harper. All were armed and looking uncharacteristically but unquestionably lethal.

She wasn't the only one to notice that the party had some late arrivals. Denny and Harlan Johnson, Junior, looked as if they'd just swallowed a persimmon berry—whole.

"Ellis and I will be takin' the boy and moseyin' along now," Bryce said with a dry smile for the brothers, regretting his earlier sense of caution and the precautions he'd taken to safeguard Ellis and the boy. He wanted very much to remove several of the brothers' teeth for them with his fists. "Unless, of course, ya got any more objections? Good. We don't expect to be hearin' from ya unless Ellis or Jonah wants to sell that land . . . and then we don't expect to hear a whole lot. Understand?"

He turned and welcomed Ellis into the bend of his long protective arm, and they started down the side of the mountain together. His truck was in sight at the bottom of the ravine before she turned to look back. Granny Yeager, with her shotgun over one arm, was the only person left to see.

"Where'd they all go?" she asked, unsure whether it hadn't been one of her fanciful dreams.

"Back to the other side of the hollow where they left their vehicles, I guess. They left town ahead of me and came through the woods the same way you did, I reckon." He helped her over an icy patch in their path.

"Ya mean ya didn't know they were there?"

"'Course I knew they were there. I ain't completely nuts. I just didn't know exactly where."

"Why didn't y'all come together?"

"I had business in town."

"The money," she guessed. "How'd ya get it?"

She'd have to know eventually—wives always did. "I mortgaged my house."

"Your . . . ?" His house. His pride and joy. His roots. His hope for the future. "Ya did that for me?"

"For you and Jonah." He shrugged as if it were nothing. "Without you, it never woulda been much of a home anyway."

Speechless, too overwhelmed with too many emotions, she waited for him to open the door of the truck and hold Jonah and the rabbit while she climbed in.

He had his arm across the back of the seat and was looking out the rear window, turning the truck around, when she asked, "How'd ya know the Johnsons would be comin' for Jonah?"

He glanced at her and grinned. "I didn't."

"Then why was everybody here? Why didn't ya come alone?"

"Simple," he said, stopping the truck and shifting into drive before he met her eyes. "I wasn't sure how much trouble I was gonna have gettin' ya to come home."

THE EDITOR'S CORNER

Next month LOVESWEPT brings you spirited heroines and to-die-for heroes in stories that explore romance in all its forms—sensuous, sweet, heartwarming, and funny. And the title of each novel is so deliciously compelling, you won't know which one to read first.

There's no better way to describe Gavin Magadan than as a **LEAN MEAN LOVING MACHINE,** LOVESWEPT #546, by Sandra Chastain, for in his boots and tight jeans he is one dangerously handsome hunk. And Stacy Lanham has made a bet to vamp him! How can she play the seducer when she's much better at replacing spark plugs than setting off sparks? Gavin shows her the way, though, when he lets himself be charmed by the lady whose lips he yearns to kiss. Sandra has created a winner with this enthralling story.

In **SLOW BURN,** LOVESWEPT #547, by Cindy Gerard, passion heats to a boiling point between Joanna Taylor and Adam Dursky. When he takes on the job of handyman in her lodge, she's drawn to a loneliness in him that echoes her own, and she longs for his strong embrace with a fierce desire. Can a redheaded rebel who's given up on love heal the pain of a tough renegade? The intensity of Cindy's writing makes this a richly emotional tale you'll long remember.

In Linda Jenkins's newest LOVESWEPT, #548, Sam Wonder *is* **MR. WONDERFUL,** a heart-stopping combination of muscles and cool sophistication. But he's furious when Trina Bartok shows up at his Ozarks resort, convinced she's just the latest candidate in his father's endless matchmaking. Still, he can't deny the sensual current that crackles between them, and when Trina makes it clear she's there only for a temporary job, he resolves to make her a permanent part of his life. Be sure not to miss this treat from Linda.

Judy Gill's offering for the month, **SUMMER LOVER**, LOVESWEPT #549, will have you thinking summer may be the most romantic season of all—although romance is the furthest thing from Donna Mailer's mind when she goes to Gray Kincaid's office to refuse his offer to buy her uncle's failing campground business. After all, the Kincaid family nearly ruined her life. But Gray's passionate persuasion soon has her sweetly surrendering amid tangled sheets. Judy's handling of this story is nothing less than superb.

Most LOVESWEPTs end with the hero and heroine happily deciding to marry, but Olivia Rupprecht, who has quickly developed a reputation for daring to be different, begins **I DO!**, #550, with Sol Standish in the Middle East and Mariah Garnett in the Midwest exchanging wedding vows through the telephone—and that's before they ever lay eyes on each other. When they finally come face-to-face, will their innocent love survive the test of harsh reality? Olivia will take your breath away with this original and stunning romance.

INTIMATE VIEW by Diane Pershing, LOVESWEPT #551, will send you flying in a whirlwind of exquisite sensation. Ben Kane certainly feels that way when he glimpses a goddess rising naked from the ocean. He resented being in a small California town to run a cable franchise until he sees Nell Pritchard and she fires his blood—enough to make him risk the danger of pursuing the solitary spitfire whose sanctuary he's invaded. Diane's second LOVE-SWEPT proves she's one of the finest newcomers to the genre.

On sale this month from FANFARE are three marvelous novels. The historical romance **HEATHER AND VELVET** showcases the exciting talent of a rising star—Teresa Medeiros. Her marvelous touch for creating memorable characters and her exquisite feel for portraying passion and emotion shine in this grand adventure of love between a bookish orphan and a notorious highwayman known as the Dreadful Scot Bandit. Ranging from the storm-swept English countryside to the wild moors of Scotland, **HEATHER AND VELVET** has garnered the following praise from *New York Times* bestselling author Amanda Quick: "A terrific tale full of larger-than-life characters and thrilling romance." Teresa Medeiros—a name to watch for.

Lush, dramatic, and poignant, **LADY HELLFIRE,** by Suzanne Robinson, is an immensely thrilling historical romance. Its hero, Alexis de Granville, Marquess of Richfield, is a cold-blooded rogue whose tragic—and possibly violent—past has hardened his heart to love . . . until he melts at the fiery touch of Kate Grey's sensual embrace.

Anna Eberhardt, whose short romances have been published under the pseudonym Tiffany White, has been nominated for *Romantic Times*'s Career Achievement award for Most Sensual Romance in a series. Now she delivers **WHISPERED HEAT,** a compelling contemporary novel of love lost, then regained. When Slader Reems is freed after five years of being wrongly imprisoned, he sets out to reclaim everything that was taken from him—including Lissa Jamison.

Also on sale this month, in the Doubleday hardcover edition, is **LIGHTNING,** by critically acclaimed Patricia Potter. During the Civil War, nobody was a better Confederate blockade runner than Englishman Adrian Cabot, but Lauren Bradley swore to stop him. Together they would be swept into passion's treacherous sea, tasting deeply of ecstasy and the danger of war.

Happy reading!

With warmest wishes,

Nita Taublib
Associate Publisher
LOVESWEPT and FANFARE

FANFARE

Now On Sale
THE FIREBIRDS
☐ 29613-2 $4.99/5.99 in Canada
by Beverly Byrne
author of THE MORGAN WOMEN

The third and final book in Beverly Byrne's remarkable trilogy of passion and revenge. The fortunes of the House of Mendoza are stunningly resolved in this contemporary romance.

FORTUNE'S CHILD
☐ 29424-5 $5.99/6.99 in Canada
by Pamela Simpson

Twenty years ago, Christina Fortune disappeared. Now she's come home to claim what's rightfully hers. But is she an heiress . . . or an imposter?

SEASON OF SHADOWS
☐ 29589-6 $5.99/6.99 in Canada
by Mary Mackey

Lucy and Cassandra were polar opposites, but from the first day they met they became the best of friends. Roommates during the turbulent sixties, they stood beside each other through fiery love affairs and heartbreaking loneliness.

🏳 　　🏳 　　🏳

THE SYMBOL OF GREAT WOMEN'S FICTION FROM BANTAM

Ask for these books at your local bookstore or use this page to order.

FN43 - 5/92

FANFARE

Rosanne Bittner

_____ 28599-8 EMBERS OF THE HEART . $4.50/5.50 in Canada
_____ 29033-9 IN THE SHADOW OF THE MOUNTAINS
$5.50/6.99 in Canada
_____ 28319-7 MONTANA WOMAN .... $4.50/5.50 in Canada
_____ 29014-2 SONG OF THE WOLF .... $4.99/5.99 in Canada

Deborah Smith

_____ 28759-1 THE BELOVED WOMAN .. $4.50/ 5.50 in Canada
_____ 29092-4 FOLLOW THE SUN .... $4.99/ 5.99 in Canada
_____ 29107-6 MIRACLE .... $4.50/ 5.50 in Canada

Tami Hoag

_____ 29053-3 MAGIC .... $3.99/4.99 in Canada

Dianne Edouard and Sandra Ware

_____ 28929-2 MORTAL SINS .... $4.99/5.99 in Canada

Kay Hooper

_____ 29256-0 THE MATCHMAKER, ... $4.50/5.50 in Canada
_____ 28953-5 STAR-CROSSED LOVERS .. $4.50/5.50 in Canada

Virginia Lynn

_____ 29257-9 CUTTER'S WOMAN, ... $4.50/4.50 in Canada
_____ 28622-6 RIVER'S DREAM, ... $3.95/4.95 in Canada

Patricia Potter

_____ 29071-1 LAWLESS .... $4.99/ 5.99 in Canada
_____ 29069-X RAINBOW .... $4.99/ 5.99 in Canada

Ask for these titles at your bookstore or use this page to order.

Please send me the books I have checked above. I am enclosing $ _____ (please add
2.50 to cover postage and handling). Send check or money order, no cash or C. O. D.'s
please.

Mr./ Ms. _____

Address _____

City/ State/ Zip _____

Send order to: Bantam Books, Dept. FN, 414 East Golf Road, Des Plaines, IL 60016
Please allow four to six weeks for delivery.
Prices and availablity subject to change without notice.   FN 17 - 4/92

FANFARE

Sandra Brown

- ❑ 28951-9 TEXAS! LUCKY .... $4.50/$5.50 in Canada
- ❑ 28990-X TEXAS! CHASE .... $4.99/$5.99 in Canada
- ❑ 29500-4 TEXAS! SAGE .... $4.99/$5.99 in Canada
- ❑ 29085-1 22 INDIGO PLACE .... $4.50/$5.50 in Canada

Amanda Quick

- ❑ 28594-7 SURRENDER .... $4.50/$5.50 in Canada
- ❑ 28932-2 SCANDAL .... $4.95/$5.95 in Canada
- ❑ 28354-5 SEDUCTION .... $4.99/$5.99 in Canada
- ❑ 29325-7 RENDEZVOUS .... $4.99/$5.99 in Canada

Deborah Smith

- ❑ 28759-1 THE BELOVED WOMAN .... $4.50/$5.50 in Canada
- ❑ 29092-4 FOLLOW THE SUN .... $4.99/$5.99 in Canada
- ❑ 29107-6 MIRACLE .... $4.50/$5.50 in Canada

Iris Johansen

- ❑ 28855-5 THE WIND DANCER .... $4.95/$5.95 in Canada
- ❑ 29032-0 STORM WINDS .... $4.99/$5.99 in Canada
- ❑ 29244-7 REAP THE WIND .... $4.99/$5.99 in Canada

Available at your local bookstore or use this page to order.

Send to: **Bantam Books, Dept. FN 18**
414 East Golf Road
Des Plaines, IL 60016

Please send me the items I have checked above. I am enclosing
$_____ (please add $2.50 to cover postage and handling). Send
check or money order, no cash or C.O.D.'s, please.

Mr./Ms._____

Address_____

City/State_____ Zip_____

Please allow four to six weeks for delivery.

Prices and availability subject to change without notice.   FN 18 1/92